THE VIKING

Typeset and printed by:
MTP Media Ltd, The Sidings, Beezon Fields, Kendal, LA9 6BL
Reg in England: 06491633
Telephone: 01539 740 937   www.mtp-media.co.uk

First published in March 2024

CONTENTS

S U P P L E M E N T S

Characters in the historical novel
Arvid
Dag/Helga
Brun/Helga
Dag

Terms used in the novel.
"Thing"   Norse parliament. All men had the right to attend.

Norse measurements

Ell	18 inches or 400 mm
Skika	Two ells or thirty-six inches
Sjomil	Sea mile — One minute of arc of the great circle, which is the Earth varying because the Earth is not a perfect sphere between 1,842 metres at the equator and 1,861 metres at the pole.
Rost	One mile
Arkriengd	One acre of arable land
Faomr	Two yards
Logey	

Norse Gods

Odin	Magician among gods and associated with runes.
Frigga	Goddess of motherhood
Thor	God of thunder, the sky, and agriculture. Odin's son
Loki	God of mischief
Balder	Son of Thor and half-brother of Thor. He had superhuman strength and was associated with light and beauty.
Hodr	Blind son of Odin

Freya	Goddess of fertility
Freyr	Associated with kingship, fertility, peace, and prosperity. Twin of Freya.
Frigg	Married to Odin. The goddess of motherhood and marriage.

Sacred plants

| Mistletoe | The only plant that could kill the god Balder. Used in Druid ceremonies. |

Norse currency

| Silver penningar | One penny |

Norse months

Morsugur	January
Porri	February
Goa	March
Einmanuor	April
Harpa	May
Skerpla	June
Solmanuor	July
Heyannir	August
Tvimanuor	September
Haustmanuor	October
Gormanuor	November
Ylir	December

Norse days

Sunnudagr	Sunday
Manadagr	Monday
Tysdagr	Tuesday
Odinsdagr	Wednesday
Porsdagr	Thursday
Frjadagr	Friday
Laugardagr	Saturday

Meals
Dagveror   breakfast
Nattveror   night meal

Crops, fruit, animals
Wheat
Barley
Rye
Oats
Peas
Millet
Flax
Hemp
Turnips
Carrots
Cabbage
Apples
Plums
Cherries
Chickens
Pigs
Cattle
Sheep
Goats
Horses
Bees
Cats
Dogs

BACKGROUND

My grandfather, Arvid, had come to this island in a raiding party nearly one hundred years ago. They had come for slaves, which they sold to royal households in their home country of Norway. My father, Dag, had served King Olaf when Olaf settled in Dublin, and he had fought under him against the native Irish tribes.

Dag brought my mother, Helga, over from Norway and four years later, Astrid was born. I came along three years later and was named Brun because of my brown eyes. In 875, I married another Helga, a young girl from my Viking tribe. Helga was beautiful, with blonde hair and bright blue eyes. We have two children, Erik and Ingrid, aged five and six. In 902, the Irish chiefs Cerball mac Murecain, the King of Leinster, and Mael Findia mac Flannacain, King of Brega, gathered thousands of their men outside the city walls. Heartened by infighting between the Vikings, they saw an opportunity to rid themselves of the Norse occupiers. It was the first day of Goa.

THE VIKING

1

E X O D U S

I peered over the city wall as thousands of Celts, many on horseback, massed outside. Some had already used ladders to climb over the edge and ran towards me. Helga screamed, grabbed Erik and Ingrid and ran towards the wharf and our small fishing boat. I turned to face the two nearest Celts, but they ran past me, following Helga. I was attacked by the Celt who followed them, a brute of a man with a red beard. I buried my sword in his stomach, but another kicked out and knocked me to the ground. I rolled over, avoiding his attack, leaping on his back while slashing my knife across his throat. I turned to follow Helga and the children, but I was too late. Helga lay slumped on the ground, blood streaming from a jagged wound in her back. She was dead. Erik and Ingrid had run to the other Norse men on the wharf, who had formed a semicircle to protect the children. I charged at the two murdering Celts, catching the first and kicking his sword away after delivering a blow to his chin with my knife. I fell on him, my knife in his chest. The younger man fled. There was nothing I could do for Helga, so I ran to join my children and the others. Erik and Ingrid were sobbing. I hugged them, and we wept together. My mother and father were not in sight.

I spotted my friend Erland and his family. We believed our chances of survival would improve in a larger boat, so we scanned the area for any available options. However, chaos reigned everywhere, with hundreds of people in the same predicament.

Sadly, we could not take our three slaves with us: Calder, who assisted me with jobs around the house; Aslos, who helped Helga in the kitchen; and a pretty young girl named Idunn, who tended the animals as well as provided me with sexual favours. (Helga did not seem to mind.) Some slaves had borne children, and it saddened me to leave one girl, in particular, I was close to behind – though we had no children. There was no time to think about this now.

They would be left to their fate, death or slavery once again.

Suddenly, amid the shouting and screaming, I spotted a longship, half full, and we ran towards it. The captain was a man I knew, Asger the Bold—we would be safe if we sailed with him. I hurried across. "Can we join you?" I shouted. "There are three of us, me and two children. We are going to Cumbria."

He replied, "We have room for you. Get in quickly."

I helped the children descend the ladder, and they clambered into the boat. I followed with my sack that contained a few bits of spare clothing, tools, silver, and food I had managed to grab. The boat quickly filled up with more families and single people. I had lost my father and mother in the melee. I looked around but could see no sign of them. It would be madness to go back. There was nothing else we could do.

Asger told me to take an oar while he gripped the rudder and told us to push off into the centre of the River Liffey, and as the current grabbed us, we gathered speed. Looking back, I could see we had departed just in time as the Celts were now pouring over the city walls. Three boatloads had gotten away, but most of the boats were left behind.

There was a southwesterly behind us, and we soon left the Liffey for the open sea as seagulls called overhead. Asger raised the sail, and we picked up a good pace. Three other boats were in sight, all heading northwest, but others in view turned west and southwest. I learned later that some of our neighbours and friends had gone to Wales, others to Cheshire, while some eventually landed in the Loire Valley in France.

I was still in a state of shock, while the children were very upset and sobbing, unable to process their mother's death. They had loved her dearly. However, my immediate concern was our safety and onward journey, and to this end, Asger asked if I could navigate. My father had taught me how to use a sundial, so I said yes. Asger pointed me to the boat's centre, where the sunstone was kept.

I set up the sandstone disc and adjustable pointer and estimated the time. The month was Einmanuor, so I could set a north-western course from the shadow formed by the vertical pointer. I shouted to Asger to adjust his course to the east. Thirty-eight people were aboard the ship, including men, women and children, and animals. There had been no time to bring cattle, but we had a few goats and sheep, a cock, and several hens, so we would have some livestock when reached Cumbria. Most families had at least two dogs and several cats locked in hazel branch cages. Frode stayed beside me. We left the peacock behind. I hope that there will be animals in Cumbria we could hunt.

We had been sailing for about four hours when Sif, who was on watch, shouted, "Land". It was the island of Mann. Asger wanted to stop over in Holmtown to take on board provisions. The helmsman steered towards the harbour. The Norse had ruled Mann for over a hundred years and had built up Holmtown's fishing industry on the plentiful shoals of herring around the island. We would be safe here.

We drew alongside the timber wharf and clambered up the ladder to the quay. Putting our feet on dry land and stretching our legs was a pleasure. Erik and Ingrid climbed out. When I told one of the older women, Agneta, what had happened to Helga, she said she would take care of my children on the voyage. She had been a friend to the family, and Erik and Ingrid were playmates with her children.

The adults gathered around Asger to decide our next step.

"I went to Cumbria a year ago. We need to head northwest again and then northeast after we pass Mann," said Asger. "We will sail another four hours, and then we will look for a spit of land which forms the entrance to a bay. We will head towards the east again, bending slightly to the north, entering a slow river we can follow until we find a suitable place to camp. It is marshy land with hazel and birch shrubs, which we can cut to make shelters for the night. Only a few Angle tribes live there. They have no reason to be hostile, so we should be left in peace to build our lives again.

"We need to buy some things here — axes, mattocks, spades. Please sort that out, Calder? Brynhild, can you buy fish? I will give you the silver. Buy anything else you will need to feed and clothe us all. It may be a week before we can buy more provisions. Brun, come with me. We need to meet the headman for any news he has."

We strolled over to where Egil was sitting outside his cottage. He had broad shoulders, a beard, and long blond hair.

"Greetings, Egil. How are you?"

"I am fine, Asger. How is it that you are here?"

Asger told him what had happened. Egil listened carefully. "I do not think they will follow you," he said. "They will be too busy looting and killing. How can I help you?"

"I am here to buy provisions and to seek your advice as you are familiar with Cumbria," responded Asger.

"You are welcome to what we can spare," said Egil. "As far as Cumbria is concerned, I would go to the least inhabited part but one with easy access to the sea and fishing. The rivers of Cumbria are filled with trout and salmon. I recommend you sail up the Solway on a tide and enter *Moricambe Bay—I will* draw you a map. You should then follow the Wampool estuary until you can go no further."

"I will do as you say," said Egil. "We shall have a feast tonight. It may be some time before we see each other again, Asger." Despite our traumas and sorrows, the night was a good one. Much ale was drunk, but we still rose early the following morning. After a quick breakfast of porridge, we walked down to the boat, said our farewells, and pushed off. We followed the coast of Mann and then bore northeast. The sea was rougher than yesterday, and some children, including Ingrid, were sick. I covered her with a woollen blanket.

After about two hours, we sighted land, gradually came closer to the coast, and followed it. We rounded a sandstone headland and held about a rost from the coastline. A dolphin rose alongside us to inspect and then slipped away again. We could see pebbled beaches and streams running into the sea. Stone cottages puffing out white smoke were scattered in groups along the beaches between the dunes and further back.

We kept on, and in an hour, we reached a promontory and passed into the bay.

The tide was running against us, so we pulled to a stop and ate the bread and cheese we had been given in Holmtown. I could see the children were upset, so I sat with them. Erik sobbed, and I put my arm around him to console the boy.

"Would you like some cheese and bread?" I asked. He nodded. Agneta passed them pieces of sheep's cheese and lumps of now dry bread. After an hour, the tide turned, and we entered the bay. We knew we had to head for the northeast corner, where a river entered. We had been told that the bay was shallow. Asger tested this with an oar and found it was two ells deep. We continued a further hour and then entered the river's estuary. It was brown in colour and slow-moving, so we lowered the sails and used the oars to take us upstream. The banks were low, with hazel, alder, and goat willow bushes. The river narrowed fairly quickly to around six ells, and Asger raised his arm and shouted that we should head for the north bank and tie up. This we did, but Erik leapt out too soon and immediately sank into the mud up to his knees. Brun and the other men in the boat laughed.

Red-faced, Erik waded ashore. I threw the rope, pulled, and walked backwards to drag the boat ashore. It was getting dark. "Let's stay the night," said Asger. "Cut branches and make a shelter. Brun, please gather kindling and light a fire. That should keep the wolves away. There will be deer in these woods tomorrow. We will see if we can shoot one, but tonight, we shall make do with what we have left." Two of the other boats had now joined us on the beach. The sheep and goats were lifted off and tethered to one of the alder trees. The hens and a cock were in the hazel branch cages strapped with leather which we placed on a patch of dry land. Afterwards, we threw them some of the corn we had brought.

I gathered the wood and got out the tinderbox with its flint to strike the steel and the amadou. After five minutes of vigorous striking, the splint sparked, and we lit the candle. Brun carried the candle to the bundle of dry wood, which was soon burning fiercely. It quickly became a large fire which, as well as frightening away the wolves and black bears, would keep us warm.

I opened what was left of our provisions of goat's cheese and bread and shared it with Erik and Ingrid. Soon, our family, now of three, crawled beneath the bear rugs we had brought. Asger had asked me to take the watch from four in the morning until daylight, so I was pleased to doze almost immediately with the children huddled beside me.

I was roused at four by Asger shaking me. "Your turn, comrade," he said. It was evident that he was tired. I rose and took his place beside the fire. It had been two days of turmoil. The violence of the Celtic attack, the murder of Helga, our flight from Dublin, the overnight stay in Mann, and the beginning of a very new life without my wife but with Ingrid and Erik to care for in a new country. What lay ahead? It was impossible to say, but we had a good group of people, and I was confident we would meet whatever situation came with bravery and strength.

I sat by the fire and sharpened my steel sword with a sandstone. I had to use my sword today but hoped I would not have to use it again. It was as well to keep it in good condition. I listened for any sounds coming through the darkness, but there were none but the occasional clucking of our hens and the bleating of our sheep. My dog Frode lay at my feet and chewed a stick. We would need to think of how to feed our animals as well as ourselves. I had not prayed for a long time but was moved to that night. I prayed to Freya, the goddess of passion and beauty. I prayed for Helga's soul, for the happiness and prosperity of my children. I thanked her for delivering the three of us from the Celts and making our settling in a new land as easy as possible.

I dozed off around 5 am and was awakened by Frode's barking. I went over to calm him and saw the source of his alarm. A large wolf was circling Frode's space beside the alder tree. I picked up a stone and threw it at the snarling animal. It caught her in the ribs, and she yelped. Frode was still excited and pulled at his chain. I stroked him, and he calmed down.

I woke Arne, a single man of around thirty with a slight limp who was next on the watchman list. I told him about the wolf. He sat by the fire while I curled up in my bear rug and went to sleep.

The cock crowed, and Asger woke us all up at 7 am. He said he would be leading a hunting party in the afternoon, hopefully, to kill a deer, and ordered, "The others need to start to build a langhus. Brun, you will be in charge." By 8 am, Asger and his men had headed off across the marsh.

I gathered my ten men and women around: "Brynhild and Agneta, will you look after the children, please? Sven, you and Arne cut down some good-sized pine trees. Bjorn, Magnus, Loki, and I will cut turves. The three of us headed inland in search of some good solid turf.

After ten minutes, we found just what we needed. We cut a rectangle twenty ells by fifty ells, which we reckoned would make a decent langhus for us all. The turves were one-third of an ell. It was hard work, but we had finished a tenth by dusk and cut and bound them with goat willow fronds. We headed back home along the same path and were soon back at the camp. Asger chose a site for the langhus on dry and raised ground. We marked the sides with a 3:4:5 triangle, and Asger ordered us to dig the turves and stack them to one side.

Five men dug the turves with mattocks while the women prepared the evening meal comprising mullet, turnip and leeks they had purchased in Mann. We cut down and trimmed over a hundred pine trees and dug pits around one ell deep and three ells apart for the pine tree trunks, which would form the structure of the walls. We would also have a beaten-earth floor with rush coverings. At 6 pm, we stopped for the day and sat down for our meal. The hunting party had not returned, but the meal was still warm, and I was not concerned. We had just finished our fish dish when there was a whoop, and Asger and his men walked into the clearing dragging a young deer. Agneta and Brynhild skinned the carcass and pulled out the intestines. They then cut steaks and put them in the frying pan with garlic, salt, and pepper.

In half an hour, the steaks were ready and were added to the plates with the turnip and leeks. We had a good first meal in our new home. Erik, Ingrid, and I said our prayers to Freya, and then I kissed them both on the forehead and tucked them into their bear rugs. They were asleep after about half an hour. My head was full of the excitement of the day and distress due to our adventures and the loss of Helga. It was some time before I drifted off to sleep.

I was woken later by the noisy chatter of sparrows and tits. Asger was already up and ready to restart building the langhus: there would be no breakfast today. I checked that Erik and Ingrid were with Agneta and joined Asger and the other men at the langhus site.

We dug pits around one ell deep and three ells apart around the rectangle. We then gathered boulders and placed the largest in four corners and the rest in between. We packed them with mud to keep the draughts out while the stone was above ground level. Next, we took the trees we had cut down, placed them vertically, and bound them with willow and aspen branches. We trampled the earth inside and strewed bracken on the floor. We were by now tired and hungry.

The women had cooked more turnips and leeks. There was venison and gravy left, and together, it made an excellent meal. After eating, we gathered around the campfire and sang Norse songs such as "My Mother Told Me" and "Lady of the Dawn". Ingrid and Erik joined in, but the air was heavy as they remembered their mother, who had sung with them before. Later in the evening, I took the children to the langhus and found them a patch of bracken to lay down close to the other children. They were both sad remembering the loss of their mother, so we said our prayers to Freya, and soon afterwards, Ingrid and Erik fell asleep. I left them and returned to the fire to talk to the other men. Asger shared his ideas with us. We needed to complete the defences and get on with the construction of the langhus as a priority. But we also needed to plant seeds and forage for plants we could eat. It was June, so we had time to gather and prepare the seeds for autumn. The women would have the task of planting them. We knew what to do tomorrow, so most of us went to bed. I joined Ingrid and Erik, and, like them, I was soon asleep.

2

V I S I T O R S

I woke up early. Tom tits were tweeting outside the langhus; a little host of sparrows had dared to come inside. But there were no crumbs for them, as the children were still asleep. What would be the future without their mother, I reflected. I would do my best, and maybe I would meet someone else. Who knows? I shrugged to myself and went outside. It was a dull day but dry. We would get on with the langhus. It would not be finished, but we should get the walls up. I wandered over to the fire. The women were making porridge and adding wood to the flames.

Agneta smiled a sympathetic smile. "How are the children?" she said.

"As well as can be expected," I replied. "It will take time."

She nodded. "It was horrible. I hate those Celts."

There was no point in going over it. It had happened, and we had to make the best of it. The men had breakfast, and half a dozen joined me at the langhus. Just then, there was a long whistle, and a group of men came out of the wood. They were blonde-haired and, if I guessed right, Saxons. One of them stepped forward and saluted us; Asger stepped forward and returned it. He spoke in their native language, and they greeted us in theirs.

"May the Gods be with you," Asger said.

"And with you," replied the Saxon.

"We come in peace," said Asger. We are Norse from Dublin, but we have fled the city since it was sacked by the Celts. "There were many casualties. We have come across the sea and landed here yesterday."

"I am Aldhelm, a bishop of Jesus Christ, and neither do we seek conflict," responded the other. "We had battles with the Celts here but overcame them, and now we only seek peace. We have a settlement at the old Roman camp near Wigton, four leagues from here. I hope we can be allies."

"That is our wish, too," responded Asger. "You must tell me about this 'Jesus Christ' sometime."

"It would be my pleasure," said Aldhelm. "You must come and feast with us at Wigton. You should follow this river for four leagues until it bears east, keep to the south and in one league, join the Roman road. Turn west, follow the Roman road for a further half a league, and you will be in the town next to our settlement and the Roman fort. We will make you welcome."

"Thank you," said Asger, "you are very kind."

Aldhelm and his men took their leave as Asger breathed a sigh of relief. He and his small group could not afford any conflict.

Asger did not know what this new religion entailed. There were many Christians in Dublin from the time of Patrick, but the Norse had always kept to the old gods. Still, there was no harm in listening to what Aldhelm and his people had to say. In the meantime, there was a langhus to build and Erik and Ingrid to care for. The men worked on the langhus until dusk when Agneta called them to their supper, which consisted of the remaining venison and vegetables.

Over the meal, we talked around the campfire about the visit from the Saxons that day.

"I am relieved they were friendly," said Asger. "We do not want any trouble as we are very vulnerable. I am not sure about this Christianity, but there is no harm in listening." Brun and the others agreed.

Brun took Erik and Ingrid to their bearskin beds in their shelter. He stayed with them for a few minutes while they said their prayers and went to sleep. He returned to the group around the campfire, and they discussed the construction of the langhus. There was general agreement that things were going in the right direction. We hoped the fair weather would continue and we all got a better night's sleep.

The following morning, we were all up bright and early. Even Erik and Ingrid were keen to help. By mealtime, the turf walls were two ells high, and a further ell had been added by supper. By tomorrow night, I thought, we should be finished, and the next phase of our journey could begin.

That night, I considered and reflected on my family's future. Usually, it would have been Helga who looked after their education. They would have learned poetry, played games such as chess, engaged in activities such as swimming and boating, and indulged in horse fighting and wrestling. Essential skills such as farming, woodcutting, carving, and metalwork could also be taught. I wondered whether any young women would be interested in helping out. I will ask Agneta tomorrow.

I rose at 6 am, intending to make an early start. It was Laugardagr, bathing day, so I asked Agneta if she could help bathe the children. I woke them up and found Agneta, who was preparing breakfast. She said she would heat water later and wash the children. I walked across to Asger, who, with a few others, was working on the langhus. He gestured to where the turves were piled up. Bring those over here, and we will add them to the walls. I did as I was asked, and all morning, we worked on digging, carting, and building with the turves. By lunch, we were at eaves' height.

The rafters were already in place, and we began to strip bark from the pine trees to make shingles. There were twenty or so of us, and we ranged throughout the nearby woodland, stripping the bark and bringing it back to the langhus. By dusk, we had the job completed. There was a hole left in the roof to allow the smoke to escape. We brought the sheep and goats into the hut and penned them in one end while dividing the inner space into rooms with posts and rails. We draped skins over the rails to give some privacy. We did well quickly, which was satisfying. Asger made a little speech saying that he was pleased with the progress we had made. We would be concentrating on planting crops and fishing. The children were cleaned up, fed by Agneta, and ready for bed. I had a few cups of ale with my friends and lay down in my new space in the corner of the room. Things were coming together.

The next day, Asger got the men together, and we started to clear an area of land to the East of the langhus. By dinner time, we had cleared enough space and harrowed and sowed the ground with the corn we had brought from Dublin. We protected the seed from the birds with hazel sprigs. It was a job well done. The next few days were spent finishing the langhus and sowing carrots, cabbage, beans, and peas. We had tried our haaf nets in the Wampool but were unsuccessful. We needed to try somewhere deeper to catch salmon and go to the coast for herring fishing. We had seen trout jumping in the river, so we would try rods and hooks to catch those. Things were generally promising.

Asger suggested that some of us should visit Wigton, make contact again with the Saxons we had met, and explore more of the hinterland. Asger chose six of us, and as instructed, we headed south along the banks of the Wampool. We could see plenty of trout in the river and resolved to catch some on our way back. We then walked on for a further league following another stream, which we learned later was the Wiza. We followed this stream along what looked like a section of the Roman road we had been told about until we settled. The six of us men approached cautiously. We did not wish to cause alarm. There was a shout, and we saw Aldhelm emerge from one of the huts. He shouted a greeting and held out his hand. Asger walked over and clasped it. All was well. Their houses were different from ours. They were square, and their walls were entirely of wood, while their roofs were pitched and clad with straw.

Aldheim asked how we were getting on. We explained how we had built our langhus and planted our crops. He thought we were making good progress. Aldheim invited us to meet the rest of the settlement. About fifty families were living there. It was built by their tribe two to three hundred years ago. It had a Christian church built next door to a market with sandstone taken from the large Roman cavalry camp about half a league away. Aldheim showed us around the church where he was the priest. He introduced me to his wife Kendra, his son Wilfred, and his daughter, a pretty, blond girl in her twenties called Megan. They were all very friendly. Aldheim suggested that our group would be welcome to stay the night.

He suggested I could stay with his family and the rest of us with other families in the village. We readily agreed, and I looked forward to getting to know him and his family better. Kendra asked me whether I liked mutton, and when I said yes, she offered to roast it for supper with vegetables. She and Megan began to prepare the supper while I followed Aldheim and Wilfred outside. I wanted to learn more about Christianity, and he told me that the founder of the religion was a Jew called Jesus who had lived in an area in the Middle East near Jerusalem eight hundred years ago. At the time, the country was under Roman rule. Jesus was understood to be the son of the one God but had been betrayed by Jewish leaders who had called for him to be crucified. He was put on the Cross alongside two robbers. Jesus preached that you should love your neighbour as yourself and love and obey your God. If you did, you would go to Heaven and be with God and Jesus forever. If you did not, you would go to Hell and burn in eternal fire. He said there would be a second coming, and Jesus would return. I tried to absorb this but felt that the old gods of Thor and Odin and the lovely Freya were more to my liking. Aldheim showed me around the church again and explained that it faced east towards the rising sun, a symbol of Jesus. There was an altar at the east end. This part of Celtic Britain had been converted to Christianity by preachers from Rome around three hundred and fifty years ago, preachers like St Patrick, St Aidan, and St Cuthbert.

I let all this sink in to reflect upon it later. Wilfred asked me questions about the battle at Dublin and was sorry to hear about Helga and sympathised with the plight of my two children. We returned to Aldhelm's house, where Kendra and Megan were about to serve supper.

We sat on benches around a wooden table. I sat between Kendra and Aldheim and opposite Megan. The food was excellent, and I complimented the ladies on it. Megan smiled and blushed faintly. I found her very attractive and hoped to get to know her better. After the first course, we had a dessert of apples and pears. Aldheim suggested we could take some young fruit plants back to start an orchard of our own. That seemed like a good idea. After taking the fruit, the men retired to the corner of the dining area while the women washed up and tidied away. Aldheim asked me further about our plans. He said that he had heard that there had been further arrivals from Dublin up the coast towards the Celtic and Roman city of Carlisle. He explained that the area of the country around Wigton was called Northumbria and under the rule of King Eadwulf, based at Bamburgh Castle.

3

A NEW BEGINNING

I had been given a room in the centre of the house, off the corridor. I excused myself, got a bearskin from a pile in the dining area, went to my room, and crawled into bed around 10 pm. I was soon asleep, but around midnight, I heard the rustle of my curtain, and a slim figure ducked in, pulled off her nightgown, and crawled under my bearskin. It was Megan; she smiled and cuddled me. I had an immediate reaction. She reached down and held my cock gently. I kissed her breasts and slipped my hand up her thighs. She groaned softly and massaged my cock. I stroked her between her legs, and she moaned louder. Gently I slipped two fingers into her cunt and stimulated the walls. We were both getting more excited. I pulled her on top of me, and she sat up and guided my penis into her cunt. I continued to massage her breasts while she rose up and down over me, slowly at first and then faster. Suddenly, she gasped and sank onto my chest. My climax followed soon after, and we both hugged each other. "Th-that was marvellous," I managed to get out, and she nodded and smiled. A few minutes later, she grabbed her nightgown, kissed me, and left.

I awoke around 8 pm, fully sated and refreshed. I had no sense of guilt but understood it would not have happened if Helga had still been alive. I stretched, threw on my tunic, and walked into the corridor to the outside door. The sun was well up in the east, just over the tops of the pine trees. I walked to the edge of the wood and relieved myself against a tree.

There was activity from a few of the other huts. Asger was out talking to Aldheim. He called me over. "I thought we should head back in the middle of the morning," he said, "as the weather looks fine. Aldheim gave me eggs and milk, and we collected a few fruit bushes and small trees. Porridge is ready for us, and most of the men are up." We went back into the hut, and I caught sight of Megan helping with the porridge. She came over, gave me a warm hug, and passed me a bowl of porridge. Aldheim could not help but notice, and I saw him exchange a knowing glance with Kendra.

During breakfast, I chatted with my friend Erland and our other Norse friends. They all appreciated the hospitality, though I had yet to learn whether their night had been as enjoyable as mine. After a few minutes, I excused myself and found Megan helping with the washing up.

"Could we have a chat before we leave?" I said.

"Of course," she said with a smile. "As soon as I have finished these pots, I will join you outside."

I walked outside and sat down on a set of wooden stocks. Megan joined me. I explained what had happened to Helga, how I had loved her very much, and how important the happiness of Erik and Ingrid was to me. Megan said she understood, liked me very much and would like to meet my children. We agreed it would be ideal if she could return to our langhus with us.

"It is new," I said, "and a bit basic, but it is the best I have."

"I am sure it will be fine," she replied, "But I need to ask my father."

"Shall I come with you?" I responded.

"I will go and speak to them both first," she said, and when I nodded, she trotted over to the hut and ducked inside.

A few minutes went by, and I began to get worried. Then her father came out and walked over to the stocks. "I should be putting you in these," he said with a wry smile. "Megan has explained that she wants to return to your camp with you. You know this means you will get married," he said firmly.

"Of course," I replied. "I want to, very much."

"I believe you," he responded, "I can see it in your eyes. She means a lot to Kendra and me."

"I know, "I said. "I love her too."

He clapped me on the back. "There is the problem of your different religions," he said. "It will be necessary for you and me to discuss this."

Kendra had been waiting with Megan, and they came across to join us. "It is all right," she murmured to Aldheim. "The main thing is that they are in love, and he is an honourable man. The religion can take care of itself."

I gathered our group together. We said our goodbyes to our Saxon friends, and we headed north to connect with another Roman road that linked the Roman fort, Maglona, near Wigton with Bowness. I squeezed Megan's hand, and we all made good progress up to the Roman road. We then followed the Wampool up to where we had landed and camped. Those who had remained, including Agneta and the children, were pleased to see us back. They were curious about Megan, and I made a point of first introducing her to Agneta, Erik, and Ingrid. Megan was charming and soon was helping with the meal and joking with the children.

Little had happened since we left. Two deer were caught and eaten, and wolves had howled in the distance, but none had come near the fire they had kept alight. No bears came near either. They had fished for trout in the river and had been successful with a brace. That night, we ate deer and vegetables. Megan and the children seemed relaxed. We relayed our stories of our meeting with the Saxons and our understanding of their Christian Church. By 9 pm, Megan, Erik, and Ingrid had retired to our room in the langhus. I had explained to the children that Megan would be sleeping with me, and they did not appear perturbed about it. That night, we made love but not as vigorously as before.

We all rose at 8 am, and Agneta and Megan prepared breakfast of porridge and fried eggs, which the children enjoyed. Asger called us together. "This morning, we will plant the fruit trees and seed Aldheim gave us. Unless anyone has a better idea, I suggest we plant the fruit trees in the land beyond the end of the langhus and the seeds we should plant on the south side of the langhus." He looked around, and people nodded their assent.

Erland and I picked up the trees and headed past the langhus. The rest of the adults grabbed the bags of seed and went to the other side. Within an hour, we planted the trees and protected them with stockades. We then tilled the soil and planted the leek, carrot, beans, and peas. We had completed all the work by 4 pm. The women then started preparing the evening meal, or Nattveror. I was pleased to see that Megan was mixing well with the others.

After our meal, Asger suggested we go out and try hunting down one or two more deer. Half of the men were interested. I decided to stay at the camp, tidy the langhus, and fish. Asger and his group left, heading up the Wampool. With Erik and Ingrid, Megan and I went back to the langhus.

We turned out the sheep, goats, and hens. "We will need to make a pen for the hens and put up some fencing for the stock," remarked Sif.

"Good idea," I said. "Let us make a start now. You and I can mark out an area for the hens and make them a nesting area. Calder and I and the others will cut down a mal of the woodland and build a fence and gate for it. It will be a field for the goats and sheep. That should take us around a week."

And so, it happened. The hen pen was constructed from hazel posts and branches, and the house from planks and main pine timbers held together with oak pegs. We completed all the construction in a day, but the field took the rest of the week. There were some loose stones that we cleared and used to make dry stone walls, but mostly, we cut down the trees and made fences by putting in two posts alongside each other and stacking the lengths of trees between, resting each length on the log in the next section to save on timber. That way, no nails were needed. The fence was two ells high, more than adequate for the sheep and goats.

During the week, we tried fishing in the Solway estuary and in the Wampool. We had brought haaf nets with us, and they now proved successful, though the others had no luck before. Each day, Sif, Garald, and Sten waded out with the haaf nets when the tide was coming in and caught salmon and sea trout. In the Wampool, we passed long nets across the and drove the fish down into them. We had dug pits in the ground near the fire pit and lined them with wood.

Each day, when the fish was fresh, the women filled pits with water and threw in hot stones from the fire. The salmon and trout were boned, and chunks of fish were thrown into the pits. Spices of dill, juniper berries, and mustard seed added. We replaced the stones regularly with fresh, hot ones. Within half an hour, the fish was ready. It was delicious with leeks, onions, and carrots. Ingrid had dug up yow yarlings, washed them and added them to the veggie stew. Megan and the other women had been making bread with the flour we had bought in Mann, so we had that with the fish. We were pleased with the fish caught in the estuary and the river.

Megan, the two children and I retired early, and after a busy day, we were soon asleep. After that, each day followed a similar pattern. We rose around 8 am, had our Dagveror, fed the hens, and collected the eggs. We then milked the goats and sheep and went fishing. In the afternoon, we did more work on the langhus and tilled the vegetables. In the evening, we had our Nattveror, or evening meal. By September, the days were getting cooler and shorter.

We had a visit from Aldheim and his friends from Wigton. They were just as friendly as before. Megan was pleased to see her father and mother again and her brother Wilfred. Aldheim told us of the great battle in Wessex in the south of the country near a large plain called Salisbury. Alfred had defeated a Danish king named Guthrum in battle. The Saxons had formed themselves into a shield wall, and the Danes were eventually routed; they surrendered and sued for peace. Guthrum promised Alfred he would leave the kingdom. He was baptised a Christian to have credibility with his Christian subjects, but he would remain a pagan to his pagan subjects. Aldheim raised his eyebrows when he said this, and Brun smiled.

"A bit like us," he said. "They also agreed on boundaries between the two peoples. Guthrum had become Alfred's adoptive son, and there had been feasting for 12 days, but now Guthrum had moved a short distance to Cirencester in Mercia and then on to East Anglia."

"All this is very interesting," said Asger, "but I hope that sort of conflict will not happen here."

Aldheim replied, "I think that a marriage between Megan and Brun will do a lot to cement the friendship between our two tribes."

"We need to talk about that," said Asger, nodding to Brun. Brun nodded back. *I shall have to find the handgeld*, thought Brun. That night, Aldheim roomed close to Asger and his wife Brenda next to Brun and Megan's room. Brun overheard them talking about the wedding. All was amicable.

Brun and Megan discussed their wedding also. It would be held at Megan's settlement as soon as possible, certainly before November. Brun would agree the handgeld with Aldheim.

"Who will be your best man?" asked Megan.

"I thought I would ask Skarde," said Brun. "You do not know him well, but we have been close since we were children. Who will you have as your bridesmaid?"

"I will ask Alva," said Megan. "She is pretty but not too pretty. She is small and elf-like, just like her name."

"Will the ceremony follow the old gods or be Christian?" asked Brun.

"We will need to think more about that," replied Megan. "I do not mind, but my mother and father may have other ideas."

Megan and I agreed on Frjadagr's day, the 13th of November, for the wedding. I set off with Skarde the following morning to travel to Wigton. I knew the way now, and we were quicker than before; it took only half a day to get there.

Aldheim greeted me warmly. "This is my best man, Skarde," I said. "We have come to discuss the date of the wedding and the handgeld."

Aldheim shook Skarde's hand warmly. "You are welcome, Skarde. Sit down, both of you and have a beaker of mead."

"We had thought about the 13th of November for the wedding," I said.

"Any reason for that date?" asked Aldheim.

"It is called Frjadagr, after Freya, the goddess of love and marriage," I responded. "Freya is also the wife of Odin, our chief god."

Aldheim smiled. "I like the sentiment, if not the reason. We can discuss the type of ceremony tomorrow. And what do you feel about the handgeld?"

"I thought about eight ounces of silver," I said.

"Megan is very pretty. I thought about twelve ounces," Aldheim replied.
After pondering, I suggested, "What say we settle at ten ounces?"

"Done," cried Aldheim. "I assume that the usual sword and shield will be handed over. I will give Megan a sword to give to you. We have a sweat lodge available for Megan. He offered his hand, which I clasped. He continued, "I wish all my dealings were as easy. Have you heard anything more about what is happening down south?" I shook my head. "No, I have heard nothing. Let us hope that we stay clear of it."

Aldheim nodded. "Come and have a few ales before we turn in." Skarde and I followed him into the langhus, where we met with the other Saxons. We had a few beers and apple ciders and then turned in for the night.

The following morning, we were up at 8 am and had a quick breakfast of porridge. We had yet to discuss the ceremony itself. We had agreed to hold it at the Roman stone Christian church called St Mary's, named after the mother of Jesus. Aldheim would officiate. It would be a simple ceremony: prayers, a blessing, and I would kiss Megan before the altar. There was nothing I disagreed with about these suggestions, so again, we shook hands.

We said our farewells and set off for home. We were back by midday. I gave Megan the news that we had concluded the arrangements for the wedding. She was naturally pleased and could continue with the planning. I told the rest of our group they were all invited, and many would attend, apart from the old and the very young.

The next few weeks were spent fishing and hunting. We explored Moricambe Bay and entered the Waver estuary. It was a river similar in size to the Wampool and entered the bay around one rost to the south. We managed to get half a rost inland and could see trout, eel, and salmon here too. The Waver looked like a suitable alternative if the Wampool failed. We caught trout and eels and took them back to the camp. We noticed that the orchard and allotment were doing well.

The women were getting excited about the wedding. Linen was dyed and sewed into dresses. I took Megan and Alva back to Wigton to have their dresses made. I returned to our encampment, which we had named Stedholme. Our blacksmith, Bjorn, had created a forge separate from the langhus. So far, he had not found any iron or copper and was using the metals he had brought with him. Soon, he intended to take a group of men to see if he could find any metal ores. I said I would go with him as I wanted to explore more. Bjorn thought we needed to go to the mountains that we could see to the southeast. We agreed to set off in a week.

Erik and Ingrid were also getting excited about the wedding and were having new clothes made. Erik had adopted a puppy he had named Ragnar after the famous warrior, and the week soon passed, and Porsdagr, named after the god of lightning, was upon us. Fifteen of us set off from the camp around 9 am. The unmarried and the very old, and some of the children stayed behind. I was sorry for them, but it was the safest that way. Hopefully, they would not be attacked by bears or wolves. There was plenty of food and lots to keep them occupied, but there were tears from some of the children.

Most of the party had yet to go to Wigton, so the journey up the Wampool and along the Roman road fascinated them. We did not visit the Roman fort, but I had told them about it and promised to take them up there on the way back. We arrived around lunchtime. Aldheim and his people greeted us warmly and ushered us to a langhus, which had been specially set aside. Megan took her wedding dress and went to stay with her mother and father. I would not see her now until tomorrow at the ceremony, set for midday. Our group settled in and made friends with the Saxons. I was staying in a special bridegroom section of the langhus. Erik and Ingrid were with me. We had an early night as tomorrow would be full on.

I woke at 7 am and reflected on the day ahead. My parent's death in Dublin came to mind. They would have loved to be here, but there was no turning back the wheels of time. This was a new start in so many ways. I gathered my sword and tunic together and went to the bathhouse to wash away my bachelor status, as was the tradition. Erik came with me!

4

T H E   W E D D

We all enjoyed our bath, dried ourselves, and dressed in our best wedding garments. Ingrid would have been doing the same in her quarters. At around 8 o'clock, we went back to our lodge. I strapped on my sword. The wedding ceremony was at 9.30. We walked to St Mary's, around a league away, near the Corn Market, accompanied by some our party, including Skarde, Asger, and the children. There was quite a crowd outside the church, and a cheer went up when they saw us. We smiled, entered the church, and took our seats at the front. Just before 9.25, Megan, her father, and Alva arrived with more cheers from the growing crowd outside. Megan and her father walked down the central passageway of the church, with Alva following. The bride, carrying a bejewelled prayer book, looked beautiful in a white dress, headdress and veil.

The simple ceremony, or wedd, was conducted by Aldheim in a white robe with gold trim and jewels. He asked me to pledge loyalty to him, and we exchanged swords. Megan read a poem she had written, and we committed ourselves to each other. Skarde produced the gold ring I had bought. I placed it on the fourth finger of Megan's left hand. We

23

kissed and walked back up the central passageway, with Skarde and Alva following.

Outside, we were greeted by the crowd around the fish market. Megan threw her flower to the crowd to a great cheer. I brandished Aldheim's sword, which was now mine, to an equal cheer. We paraded through the town with local people throwing cakes at us. We returned to the Stedholme langhus, which would be our permanent home. We arrived around evening mealtime as planned. Agnetha and friends were pleased to see us. And keen to hear the news. Megan apprised them enthusiastically, but we were all tired, especially the children, and headed early to our beds.

The following morning, we rose at 8:30. We all grabbed our breakfast of porridge and fruit. I set off early to see the progress made in our absence. The garden was well weeded. The fruit trees had taken well, particularly the small apples. The sheep and goats continued to be milked, and the hens and ducks gave eggs. I grabbed a handful of Agnetha's crusty bread, and I went to the river and put a wicker skiff into the stream. I had taken my net and scooped up a catch of smaller fish, which I brought back to the langhus. Megan filleted them and roasted them in the embers beside the fire. I had laid my new sword by my side at night and now showed it to the men in our hamlet. Skarde and I told our fellows about the excellent hospitality we received. They liked my other sword, but they liked this too. I hoped to put it to good use.

Asger called all the men together in the centre of our settlement. "We have enjoyed ourselves," he said, "but I am pleased to be home. We have made new friends, and we will continue to meet up from time to time. Our young men and women, and maybe some old ones, will acquire new spouses. However, you will have heard that the Saxons defeated the Danes recently in the south, and Guthrum had sued for peace. We need to be aware of new developments all the time. It is a good place here. We have fish, and we are beginning to establish a farm and orchard, but we need to think about our defences. We are sheltered by the sea and hidden from the west, but I have considered building stockades to the north and south. I want volunteers to start cutting down and stripping the trees this afternoon." The men nodded.

"I will go," said Warg.

"I, too." said both Bjorn and Odjer.

After two more raised their hands, we set off immediately, with Skarde leading the way. On Asger's orders, the remainder of the men and boys would work the garden and fish.

We headed north of the camp into an area which was new to us. The land was drier, with the same oak, beech, ash, and lime but more Scots pine, one of which Skarde singled out. "We will start here by felling this tree and stripping its branches. We should be able to split the lower trunk and then get about four more staves from the upper lengths. We can point them out later today when we return to camp." This we did without mishap, and we repeated this pattern for ten days, by which time we had enough trees to complete a stockade of seven longeyrir long and four ells wide. There was a raised platform on the inside to give the defenders the height to hurl spears down on the assailants and to pour boiling water on them.

Life progressed comfortably through the autumn, and we began to think about Yule. This was a big festival for us Norse. There would be banquets and sacrifices to the gods and the ancestors for twelve days. Odin was our most revered god. He brought gifts, and we sacrificed goats for him. We offer a kid goat in honour of Saturn, the god of agriculture and richness. The festival marks the turning of the sun and the return of the good times. It was also the time for Megan and me to expect our first child, in Morsugr, so it would be doubly exciting.

5

THE RAID

We continued with our hunting, fishing and tilling. The vegetable and fruit bushes had done well, and we had a good harvest. One morning, I heard a shout from Loki; he had been collecting mussels down by the shore and was pointing out to sea. I looked across and could see three sails of our ships on the horizon. They were heading towards us. Asger shouted to close the gates and for the men to take their position on the ramparts. Each of us had a job to do. The mothers and children went to the langhus, and Agneta and the other women boiled water to throw onto any invader. One Alva, the elf, who was very brave, picked up a sword and was ready to fight hand-to-hand. The men and boys headed to the ramparts to prepare for repelling invaders.

The sails were making quick progress and had entered the Wampool estuary, approaching the mooring points. Although the newcomers were Vikings, that did not mean they were friendly. Asger stood on the rampart next to the gate and waited. We saw that the men had landed on our port side and were surveying us from around two hundred ells away.

Forty of them, young to mature men, discussed the situation. One of them took the lead and headed up the river towards the enclosure. They looked anything but friendly. Thirty spread out about twenty ells in front of the stockade wall. The others, the older ones, stayed by the three boats. The leader, a tall man with a red beard, raised and then dropped his arm. The thirty men charged at us, screaming.

Our arrows took down six of them, including their red-bearded leader. But most reached the wall to scale it. Two fell, speared by our men, and I severed an invader's head as the women threw boiling water over the others, who fled screaming. The wounded managed to return to the boats. A dozen or so climbed the fence and fought hand-to-hand with our men. It was a vicious fight.

The women and children had barricaded themselves into the langhus, though Alva remained outside, brandishing her sword. I could see Asger was leading a group of men on the other side of the stockade. The man I was facing was blond and sturdy. He grinned and crashed his sword towards me. I defended myself with my shield as best I could. Skarde put his opponent to the sword and then attacked another. I received a slight wound to my side but thrust my sword upwards into my opponent's groin. He fell to the ground with a scream. I finished him off by plunging my sword through his chest. We were gradually gaining the upper hand.

The shout for retreat was raised, and the leader and ten of his men jumped the stockade down to the other side. We concentrated on finishing off those.

Tragically, we had lost six men, but most and all the women and children had survived. Megan and the children rushed from the langhus to embrace us, shaking and weeping. Megan bandaged my wound as the others were likewise cared for. Alva, the one woman who had fought, had lost her hand at the wrist and was bleeding profusely. She held it up and grimaced. Asger tried to comfort her as best he could. He gestured to Agnetha to take care of her. We climbed the stockade and watched as the remainder of our attackers tended their wounded, then sailed out into the estuary and headed north up the coast.

"It could have been worse," I told Megan and Skarde. "Let us bury the dead."

First, we gathered our dead together and laid them out beside each other in a row. There were six. According to custom, we would burn them on a funeral pyre. Under Asger's instruction, we constructed a pile of stones in the centre of the camp. We then gathered heather and wood and piled them on the stones. The bodies were then carefully lifted onto the pyre. Asger lit a torch of dried grass and twigs and set the pyre alight. The wives and children of the men wept. We all filed past and saluted the bodies. The smoke carried the souls of the warriors to Valhalla.

After cremation, their ashes were buried in a hole in the ground some distance away from the settlement, all under Asger's watchful eye. Their weapons were buried with them, together with their clothes and ornaments, which their wives had brought together. A pile of stones then covered the grave. We believed their souls would be going to Valhalla as befitted those who had died in battle. It was then the turn of our former enemies, treated in the same way, though buried in a separate mound. We were unsure where their souls would go, but it would not be Valhalla, but a lesser place known as Hel.

That night was a sombre affair. Megan and I helped cook a supper of venison for the tribe. We discussed the attack, its motivation, whether it could happen again and those we had lost. Our fortifications had stayed strong, and we were lucky that we had erected them in time. Tomorrow, we will conduct necessary repairs and make any improvements we need. We then said our thanks to Thor and Megan to her Christian god. Agnetha put the children to sleep while Megan and I curled up by the fire.

In the morning, we woke around 7.30, surprisingly refreshed. Agnetha helped Megan dress the children, and we then had our breakfast of porridge. I joined Skarde and Asger to inspect the damage. It was minimal as there had been no fire, which is the worst. We gathered the enemy swords left behind and put them in the langhus. We would think further about any improvements we wanted to make to the defences. I went down to the estuary, but there was no sign of our foes. "They will be back," pronounced Asger, "and this time with more men and equipment. We will have to be ready." We all agreed. In the meantime, we would live much as we had before, hunting, fishing, and managing our crops.

I went out to inspect my onions, leeks and carrots. Megan and I thought that it would be a good idea for Erik and Ingrid to have a puppy to look after. One of the Buhunds brought over on the boat had recently had a litter of six pups. I asked the owner, Arne, if I could have one, and he agreed. I took Erik and Ingrid to see them in their pen next to the langhus.

"I like that one," said Erik, pointing to a sweet pup with a waggy tail.

"I do, too," said Ingrid.

Arne and I agreed on a price of ten penningars. I made a collar and lead, and Erik brought it back to our section of the langhus, where they proceeded to pet and play with it. A good move, I thought. They named the puppy Thor.

6

It was now the fifth day of Gormanuor, and the baby was due in seven months, in Skerpla. Before then, we had Yule, which started on the shortest day the twenty-first of the month of Ylir. It would be the first Viking winter for Megan and the first for the children without their mother. Before then, there was lots to do on the land; there would be crops to harvest, animals to fatten, fish to catch, smoke, salt, dry, pickle ferment in whey as my mother used to do. Six of the women were pregnant, so there would be a lot going on over the next year.

We continued building up our defences; the last raid had given us a scare. We held a Council led by Asger when we agreed to raise the palisade by two ells, with more pointed young pine trees strapped to the existing rampart pointing outwards. Asger would take charge of a team of men to carry that out. We decided to extend the eastern side of the stockade to cater for the increasing number of animals and people we were accruing. A new main gate was to be built in that eastern wall. I was to take charge of the extension. We needed more crop space and an orchard garden, which we would cultivate in the extension. Agneta would be in charge here. The langhus would need to be extended, and Skarde would lead a team to construct this. Time flew by. Megan and I were incredibly happy, and Erik and Ingrid enjoyed house training and playing with Thor, the name they had given their puppy. She slept beside them in the langhus. It was working well.

Much of this work had been done by the first day of Gormanuor. The fruit had been harvested, fish caught, salted and smoked, and stored on racks. We would eat wild boar on the night of the main feast, the winter solstice, and three of those were fattening up nicely. Asger decided we needed a break and thought a trip to Olenacum, the old Roman fort just south of Wigton, would be enjoyable. Half of us would go – men, women, and their children – while the others would remain to look after our encampment. The men drew lots, and the winning twenty would go with their families. Come the summer, the other half would go. I drew one of the lucky long straws so we would go the following Mandag, in three days' time.

It soon came around, and Asger and his family led us out of the camp. Although Megan and I had been along the route many times, the children had not. We had decided to bring Inga along; she thought it was a great adventure. We followed the Wampool as usual, then cut across to Wigton, where we called to see Aldhelm and his tribe. All was well with them, and it seemed to me from the reactions of our single men to the women and girls there that there may be romance amongst them in the future.

We now headed south past the church and cottages, up the hill to the Roman road and the ruined fort and settlement at the top. We headed to the fort, where foundations and low walls were sticking out of the grazing fields. The farms nearest to the fort, which we passed, and others we could see a rost or so away, were constructed from the same sandstone as the fort and the church in the town. Many of them had pieces of Roman statues embedded in their walls.

Walking around the fort was a true experience. The Roman road we were following led through what looked like a gate; similarly, an east-west road went through some kind of parade ground. The fort was above the stream which flowed below and to the west. So, water must have had to be carried up twenty or so faomrs to get to the buildings.

This would have been quite a job, considering there would have been a cohort of one thousand troops stationed there. Still, I suppose they had plenty of Celtic slaves. It was strategically located with roads heading east and west, north, and south. The children and the dog played on the grass while the adults wandered around thoughtfully. We knew all about the Romans; they had conquered Britain in the early first century and brought civilization of a kind to the Celtic peoples—for almost four hundred years in Britain! Ports, towns, roads and country villas were built. New animals, hares, cats, snails and rabbits were introduced, and birds such as peacocks, pheasants and guinea fowl were kept. Vegetables were also planted, including cabbages, peas, celery, turnips, parsnips, onions and radishes. Fruit trees, plums, pears, walnuts and cherries were planted in orchards. Plants imported included lilies, violets, pansies, poppies and nettles. An amazing change in civilization happened. Then it all went wrong! Rome fell to the Huns, and the Roman Empire was over. The Romans and their followers left Britain around four hundred years ago. Gradually, Picts took over the north of Cumbria, crossing Hadrian's Wall and spreading south. Saxons came from Eastern Europe, and we, the Norse, have come from Norway and latterly from Ireland.

A handful of occupants of the surrounding farms came across to see us. Cautiously, they began to engage with us when they could see we meant no harm and had women and children with us. They were a blue-eyed people of Saxon descent, so Megan could engage easily with them. They were keen to have news of what was happening in the rest of England, and we told them what we knew about Alfred and his battles.

The sun was beginning to set when we left to return to Wigton, where we had told Aldheim we would stay after our visit to the fort. It had been a remarkably interesting experience and gave Megan and me much food for thought. What would the future be for our tribes? Would we finish up like the Romans? We talked it through with Aldheim and the others of his tribe. But none of us knew the answer. "It is the choice of God," said Aldheim. "Everything is planned, and we expect there will be a second coming, Jesus the son of God will return, and there will be heaven on earth. That is what we believe." *Maybe*, I thought, but as far as I could see, the desires and spirit of man played a big part in history, and we had to do as much as we could ourselves to safeguard our future. My own life history to date made that plain to me.

The following morning, we set off back to our home, and we got back by lunchtime. Agnetha and her friends were pleased to see us. Nothing untoward had happened—no sign of any more invaders. We carried on as before, fishing, hunting, looking after the stock and plants and trees. We gradually felled more trees and expanded the area of our vegetable patch and orchard. We vowed that our next trip would be to the mountains, the old Roman town of Luguvalium and then down the coast to the Roman post and fort of Alavna and beyond. We were getting to know the place, and we were beginning to think of it as home.

First though there was Yule in fourteen days' time. We had holly and mistletoe to pick, evergreen branches to cut, animals to sacrifice and gifts and wreaths to make. We would have to procure some bells. Asger put Agnetha in charge; he knew she enjoyed festivities. Five went to the woods to collect the items to decorate our homes. There was much to do.

The main meal would be based on wild boar. I was asked to hunt and kill the boar on Yule Eve and bring it home for cooking. There would be turnips, leeks and carrots. Gravy would be made from the boar's entrails. The pudding would consist of cranberries and other fruits in a wheat flour pudding and white sauce with brandy. I could taste it now.

Megan was used to a very similar Yule, and she enthusiastically joined in with Agnetha and the rest of the women and children. I had made Erik a bow and a quiver of arrows, and Megan had made Ingrid a dress of linen with ribbons of red, green and gold. We kept the presents secret from the children as was the custom. The night before Yule, all the children were excited, wondering what they would get as presents and looking forward to the festival. Eventually, they did get to sleep. We put their presents under the mistletoe where they lay. We joined the adults, drinking beer and singing. A huge oak log had been brought into the langhus and decorated with holly, juniper and mistletoe. It was a tradition that it be lit with a piece of wood kept from last year. This would not be possible this year. Hopefully, next year. The log was soon burning strongly. This activity symbolised the creation of light where there was darkness. The burning and the smoke produced would drive evil spirits from the house. Prayers were sent by Asger to Odin for the rising of the sun, and then the ale began to flow. This was all new to Megan, who had a Christian Christmas and was celebrating the birth of Christ. Around midnight, Megan and I excused ourselves and slipped away. The festivities were kept going by the younger ones.

We were woken around 7.30 am by shouts of delight from children all around the langhus. Ingrid and Erik were delighted with their presents and thanked us both. They gave us presents –scented lotion for Megan and a linen shirt that Megan had made for me. We were delighted and thanked them warmly. We all trooped off for breakfast in our new gear and lotion. The scene was replicated all around the langhus. Agnetha was bustling about ensuring the meal would be ready on time, checking that the wild boar would be tender while the other women prepared the vegetables. The food was served on wooden platters and eaten with steel hand-forged cutlery. The beer, mead, saliva and a little wine imported from France were served in bone drinking horns. The children drank weak beer. As well as the wild boar, we had turnips, cabbages and carrots. For dessert, we had fruit pudding.

It was a jolly affair. Asger led the singing of Viking songs, Sif played the lyre, and I played the jaw harp. Men, women and children joined in and even the babies chortled. After midnight, we all retired. The following morning, we all slept in, even the children. It was around 10.00 am when I walked out of the langhus. A few people were milling around, but it was going to be a quiet day. Megan rose and got the children up. They were a bit bleary-eyed, but Ingrid was proud of her new shirt and would show it off to her friends. Erik was practising with his bow and arrows. He had set up a target of wool on a tree. I went to help him. He was pleased with the attention and was doing well.

Asger was doing the tour of the langhus, seeing how people were. He asked us what our aspirations were for ourselves and our children. Most mentioned the need for more security and education for the children. Asger promised to attend to the security and consulted Agnetha about education. Agnetha was well-educated and had already given thought to the problem. She said, "Both the girls and boys should learn their runic alphabet and use it to carve messages on stones. They should learn to understand poetry and how to write it. The boys should learn martial arts to a high standard, including how to wrestle and fight with their fists and with spears, axes and swords. How to make and use bows and arrows is important. They should know how to make oil lamps. Both sexes should also learn how to ride horses and row and sail. The girls should learn how to use a loom. They will be working on this every day. They must learn to make cheese, milk cows, sheep and goats and look after hens, geese and ducks. They must know about our gods and their importance, particularly Odin and Freya. Megan will want her children to know about Christianity and other religions, such as Islam.

"There is a lot to learn," said Agneta. Asger nodded thoughtfully. "But I am prepared to help," added Megan helpfully.

"Good," said Asger, "but you will need others."

"Aslaug and Brenda would be suitable to teach about our gods, and Megan would help with Christianity. Skarde would enjoy teaching martial arts, riding and rowing. Brun could teach navigation and Ojer how to look after animals, plants and trees."

"I did not realise we had so many skilful people," responded Asger. "I shall leave you in charge, Agnetha, and thank you. Please come to me if you need any help."

"I will," replied Agnetha. Determinedly, she set off to start on it right away.

Asger told Brun and others what he had agreed with Agnetha. Good thought Brun, but it is a big job, and she will have her work cut out. Brun explained to Erik and Ingrid what Asger and Agnetha had agreed, and they were very enthusiastic. One hundred and seventy-five of us had landed in Cumbria. We had lost six in the fight with the other Vikings. That left one hundred and sixty-nine. Of these, fifty-nine were children of school age. There were twenty-five boys and thirty-four girls—a big class they might have to split into two. Not my job, though, thank goodness, thought Brun. *I shall stick to navigation.*

I went back to helping Erik with his archery, and soon, it was time for our midday meal. There was plenty left from the festivities to last a couple of days, so we had the warmed-up boar and veg.

In the afternoon, we went for a family walk down to the Wampool, took out a boat to fish. It was calm but cold, and we did not stay out long. We did not catch anything. When we got back, Agnetha had already started on her education plan. She had divided the children into two classes, thirty in one and twenty-nine in the other. Erik and Ingrid were in the same class, and Agnetha had recruited Brona, one of the younger women, to take charge of their class. I knew her from Dublin; she was personable, and I thought she would be an excellent teacher. Erik and Ingrid were enthusiastic and keen to start. Agnetha planned to begin classes in a week's time, just before the end of the winter solstice. She needed time to prepare the timetable and gather all the implements and their storage together. I would be concentrating on hunting, fishing, and helping Asger with completing the work on the defences.

Some of our young men and women had formed relationships with people from Aldhelm's tribe, and there were many weddings to attend, which were very enjoyable. Megan made the journey several times to meet with family and friends, sometimes on foot, but now more frequently by horseback. There were no other tribes spotted in the area or visitors from across the sea. A few of us made a special trip by sea up the coast and the Eden Estuary to the large Roman town of Luguvalium. We berthed on the north side of Eden Bridge and walked over the bridge and up to the marketplace and the town centre. The market was bustling with locals and travellers selling all kinds of goods. It was smaller than Dublin but similar in character with a city wall, an attractive sandstone church with a square tower and stained-glass windows. Caer Luel was on an oppidum constructed by the Celts to provide a safe building where they could retreat in case of attack. Later, the Romans made this a flourishing town, with baths and aqueducts, pivotal for coordinating activities along the west side of the Roman wall. After the Romans came Old King Cole, who is still sung about, ruled over a massive kingdom from the River Mersey to Hadrian's Wall. After King Cole, the kingdom split into a patchwork of smaller kingdoms. Cumbria was ruled by Urien, who held his court in Caer Luel. He attracted talented people to Caer Luel, including the bard Taliesin. It was a turbulent time, with Urien engaged in constant wars.

Unfortunately, Urien aroused jealousy and was murdered by another king, Morcant. Owain, Urien's son, took over from his father, but he died a few years later, and he, in turn, was succeeded by his brother Rhun, who was succeeded by his son Roedd. Later, around two hundred years ago, their kingdom was absorbed into Northumbria. Owain had an illegitimate son who later became Christian St Mungo. Many stories are told about this turbulent period of Cumbrian history, and I learned them even in Dublin. The stories of King Arthur and the Round Table are linked to this period and Cumbria. It isn't easy, though, to separate the facts from fiction. I was pleased that now, in Cumbria, it was generally quieter, but you never knew when violence could break out.

The Celts, though, did exist and their mathematical knowledge and accomplishments of building roads and towns right across Europe is as impressive as was the Romans one thousand years later. We, the Norse, had captured Caer Luel and sacked it in the year 876, and we held it still, but the Saxons, I understood, had designs on it. I would keep out of that problem.

Asger led us back down to the river the following morning, and we were back into the Sulwath in two hours and up into Moricambe Bay in four hours. We got back to our camp in the early evening. On the way, we talked about naming our encampment. We decided on Stedholme, or "farm on an island of raised land". It sounded good.

It was now the month of Porri, and the baby would be due in Harpa in three months. Megan was still looking healthy, eating, and sleeping well. So far, nothing to worry about. I thought it would be interesting to take a trip by boat down the coast for a day or two. I mentioned it to Asger, but he preferred to stay at home. My best man, Skarde had married one of our Norse girls, Liv, and was busy, but Bjorn, Calder, Erland and Arne were up for it, so we planned to set off the following week.

We planned our provisions and opted to take a smaller boat we had under construction. The sails were to be finished, and Megan was working on those. I had to finish the woodwork, and Bjorn was helping me with that. Everything was ready by Sunnudagr, the day before we were due to set off, and we went out for a trial sail. Minor adjustments to the tiller were necessary, but, otherwise, it was fine.

The following morning, we set off with the best wishes of the crowd who had come to see us off. The weather was fine as we rowed down the river to the bay and then out into the estuary. We were sailing against the prevailing wind as we headed down the coast past the herring fishing village, whose inhabitants waved to us as they mended their nets on the beach. We passed by a Roman fortlet on a hill near the shore and then came to the river estuary. Overlooking the sea was a sandstone work which was a major Roman fort and nearby town. We sailed into the estuary and came upon a port. We understood from Aldheim that this was a major Roman port called Alauna. We entered the estuary and tied up alongside the dock. There were other boats with men working on them. No one seemed bothered by us. It was as though they saw Viking longboats every day. We went over to talk to a couple of men working on another longboat. To our amazement, they were Vikings and spoke a similar dialect to us. They were called Sune and Thorwall, and they had fled from Dublin at the same time as us and landed here. We told them our story, and they promised to visit us. They told us Alauna traded with the Norse in Mann, mainly in herring. The Romans established it shortly after arriving in Cumbria around six hundred years ago. The first commander, Marcus Agrippa, a close friend of the emperor Hadrian, had stationed a mounted unit of five hundred men here. They heralded from the north Rhine area. When Rome fell, they returned to Germany, and the land had been left uninhabited until a few Saxons came to farm and fish here around three hundred years ago, and then the Norse escapees had arrived this year.

We walked up to the town on the heights and admired the ruins. Broken pottery was lying around, and sandstone altars, but there were no intact buildings. We walked back down to the port. We talked a little more with Sune and Thorwall, who were still there. We invited them to visit us in Stedholme, and they said they would.

I bought gifts of cloth for Megan and Agnetha, a brooch for Ingrid and a leather football for Erik, which I knew he had never seen before. I also bought baby clothes for the new arrival. We then boarded the boat and set sail. We decided to head south to where we had been told there was a major Roman port. It was a fair journey of some thirty rosts, which took six hours altogether. We could see Mann to the west and the mountains to the east. We saw no sign of forts or other defences apart from those at the estuary of a large river about two hours south of Alauna. We landed there and found a large Roman fort north of the settlement. We had a quick look around but could not see much. I promised to return when I had more time. We finally arrived at

Ravenglass in the evening. It was a large estuary with a magnificent port at its heart. Although many of the buildings had been destroyed, one villa was intact and occupied by a young Viking family, who were pleased to see us. Like us, they had come from Ireland, south of Dublin. The Celts had killed their parents, but they had hidden in the woods and then gone down to the beach at night, stolen a boat and made it across here.

They had been lucky to come across this empty villa and had a good life fishing and hunting. The villa's windows had retained their glass, and the walls were still covered in the original pink lime plaster. They had found much Roman debris, glazed clay containers used to bring wine from the continent and pieces of stone engravings. We stayed here in relative luxury for two nights before heading back home. We arrived in Stedholme late afternoon and were heartily greeted by our families. Megan was delighted with the linen material I had brought, Ingrid with her brooch and Erik with his football. He was soon kicking it around with his friends. I took Agnetha her linen, and she was pleased with it. The other men had had the same reactions. Megan put the baby clothes away. I hope we were not being premature.

7

T H E   B I R T H

Megan and I made love gently but insistently that night. We were still very much in love. The following morning, we rose late. It had been a strenuous few days, and I needed a rest. Erik wanted me to kick the football around with him, which I did, and then I persuaded him to join his friends. I hoped it would be an easy day.

The baby was due early in Harpa, and it was now the end of Goa. It would be here in two months. Agnetha would be the midwife and had everything she needed. We were ready. A section was portioned off with posts, hemp rope, and skins in one corner of the langhus. We had done all we could. Megan began to contract around midnight, and I raised Agnetha. I boiled water in a metal pot on the fire while Agnetha soothed Megan's brow. Megan was grimacing. I moved beside her and held her hand.

The contractions were becoming more frequent. Agnetha, though, had seen it all before. She continued to wipe Megan's brow. After ten minutes, the contractions and Megan's breathing became more frequent. Agnetha sang a Viking children's song, but I did not know the words, so

I hummed along. Megan squeezed my hand even more tightly. Suddenly, she gasped, and I could see the crown of a head. Megan kept pushing, and the body began to be pushed out, and then the legs. Megan's face was contorted with pain. "One last push," said Agnetha encouragingly, and then it was over. The baby was born.

"It's a boy," said Agnetha with a smile.

"Well done, Megan," I said and embraced her.

Agnetha washed the baby in warm water and dried it with clean towels. Megan reached over and took the baby from Agnetha, pulled it to her left nipple, and the baby immediately began to suckle.

"What will he be called?" asked Agnetha. "We had thought Dag after my father," I said.

"That is nice," said Agnetha.

I went outside into the main part of the langhus and announced Dag's birth to the throng. "Congratulations," shouted Asger and waved the sword he had been sharpening. Others did the same.

Skarde came over and clasped my hand. "Well done, brother," he said. "One day, it will be my turn." I knew he had been seeing one of the Saxon girls, Collibe, and I thought, *it would not be long.*

I went back inside. Megan was still feeding Dag, and Agnetha was putting away the cloths. "Could you empty the basin, please?" she asked, and I took it from her and emptied it in the hazel bushes outside the tent. I went back inside and watched as Megan stood up and rocked Dag backwards and forwards. He looked as though he would soon be asleep. There was nothing for me to do. It was now 3 am and time for me to get some sleep. I kissed Megan on the cheek, lay down on our rug and pulled another rug on top. I gradually went to sleep, smiling.

I was woken up by Dag crying around 7 am. Megan was already up, and she had been outside and had a wash. She smiled, and I gave her a hug and kiss. Dag was in his cradle and ready for another feed. Megan picked him up and then sat down and put him to her right nipple. He sucked greedily. "He is going to be a strong lad," I said, stroking his head. "I shall leave you now and see what Asger is doing." Megan nodded, and I left our enclosure and walked out of the langhus.

8

MAKING THINGS SAFER
AND
SOME NEW VISITORS

Asger had a group of men around him, and I joined them. Two men were positioned all day by the river, keeping guard against any further attack. "We are going to do some more work on the fortifications," Asger said. "Would you like to join us?"

"Sure," I said, "I can help today."

"I thought we would start at the gates, divide into two parties and work around the river. We could meet there and have something to eat. I have two sets of tools, including axes and rope. I want you to take your time and repair any damaged areas and add to them where necessary in terms of height and thickness." We nodded. I had Skarde, Avery, Chad and Edgar in my group. I took charge, and we started off at the gate. Asger's group had gone to the north side and were repairing a section of the wall. The gate needed extra hinges on each side in the centre. There were two, which Bjorn the blacksmith had made for the job, and Skarde and Chad set to work fixing them to the inside of the gate.

Avery, Edgar, and I examined the wall south of the gate. We climbed up onto the platform using the ladders and looked down. The wall and the platform were in good condition. It was high enough and wide enough. We needed to ensure that the armaments—bows and arrows, small boulders, and pots of water—were plentiful. Skarde said he would see to that, and the rest of us worked around the wall. The remainder of the wall was in good shape, so when we got to the river, I decided to head back to the langhus, leaving the rest of the men to talk to the guards. Megan and Dag were waiting, and we sat together by the fire.

Later, Megan and I had supper of leek soup and bread rolls prepared by Agneta. It was delicious. Later, Megan, Dag, and I walked down to the river. It was cold, so we did not stay out long. When we returned, Megan fed Dag and put him down to sleep. Megan and I curled up beneath our bearskins, and we, too, were soon asleep.

Another day. After breakfast, I reported to Asger while Megan fed and cared for Dag. With our defences reinforced and a watch in place, the attention now shifted to building up our settlement. We chopped down more trees and uprooted the stumps to create more grazing land. We planned to go on an expedition into the mountains soon, which was exciting as we knew we would encounter wolves and bears.

One morning, we had an enormous and joyous surprise. Who should walk into our compound but my parents, Dag and Helga, and two other couples we had last seen in Dublin. They had escaped the city by boat and travelled across the Irish Sea to land up the coast to the north of the Solway. They had then travelled up the River Annan and had settled there. They had heard on the grapevine that there were Norse people on the south side of the estuary and had taken the trip across the Solway by wading over the Sulwath from Annan to the Roman fort at Bowness. There, they had heard about a group of Norse living in Moricambe Bay on the Wampool. They had walked across the common to the Wampool and then followed it to where we were. It was marvellous to see them and their friends, and, of course, they were delighted to meet Megan and Dag number two and our friends. Asger made them all very welcome. We found a space for them to sleep next to us. They told all of us their stories, and we told them ours. Their settlement near the Annan was less advanced than ours, so it made sense for them to stay with us at Stedholme. Asger agreed, and so it happened. My mother was delighted with her new grandson and Megan, and I could see that it would all work out. Helga took over Agnetha's duties, giving her more time to educate and train the children. The adjustment was complete, and everyone was happy.

Later, Dag Senior said he would like to join us on our journey into the nearby mountains. He was also keen to learn about the wars in the south and Alfred's defeat of the Norse at the battle of Ashdown in 870. Since then, the Vikings have been the dominant force in the country. "Quite honestly," said Asger, "we are better keeping out of the politics and getting on with our own lives." Megan and I nodded as we were the product of that. I explained about the differences in our religions. They had heard about Christianity from other sources and understood. We told them about Aldheim, the settlement of Wigton, and the Christian church there. They could see that the religious differences were no problem for Megan and me.

We all went to bed happy but with much to think about. The following morning, I introduced my father and his friends, Wors and Frigg and Toke and Freydis, to the Norse who were here. Wors and Toke were keen to participate fully in our life here. I showed them our defences and explained why they had been built. They were a bit shocked to learn that it was a Viking group who had attacked us.

They assisted us with felling the trees and clearing the ground and helped Erik and the other boys with their football. On Sunnudagr, we got ready for the journey to the mountains the following day. We needed provisions, weapons and sturdy footwear. I was to lead the expedition, and we set off at 9 am the next morning. We followed our usual route up the Wampool to the Roman road and then to Wigton and along the Roman road to Torpenhow, which means hill in three languages—Saxon, Welsh and Norse. We turned south here, and the six of us—myself, my father, my father's friends Wors and Toke and my friends Skarde and Chad—headed up the bracken slope.

After a walk of two rosts, we reached an area of stonework that had all the appearance of a Roman fort. It looked all the way down to the Sulwath. We poked around, but there was nothing of interest or value, so we pushed on, still climbing. There were a few very remote farmhouses with many sheep. After two more rosts, we looked down to a beautiful lake. We stopped to enjoy the view and then walked down towards the water. A large river flowed from the lake, and we headed towards where it joined it. Crossing it would have been tricky, so we headed down the east side of the lake. There were large deciduous trees on each side of the valley. Above the tree line to the east, a large mountain towered above us, with its top covered in snow. There were farms in the valley, and where people were working in the fields alongside the farm buildings, we called out to them. They waved cautiously back. They looked Saxon, with tidy blond hair. When they seemed willing to talk, we told them our recent history. They seemed sympathetic. They had no love for the Celts.

The walk down the valley alongside the lake was exhilarating. Eagles and buzzards flew overhead. There were squirrels in the clumps of pine, which were becoming more frequent; occasionally, we saw deer and wolves. We came to the end of the lake, and there was then a marshy area with cattle grazing. Beyond the lake, we followed a road or broad path, possibly Roman. It led us to a cluster of houses from which people emerged. My father, Skarde and I walked forward to greet them. They were Saxon in appearance. We told them who we were and where we had come from. They seemed unsure of us until we mentioned Aldheim and Wigton when they warmed up, and their chief invited us into his home. It was quite small and had a roof of rushes. Its sides were of wooden planks. He said his name was Cuthbert, like the Christian preacher. His wife's name was Mildred. They had three children who surrounded us and listened to the conversation. We told Cuthbert where we had settled and why.

He said his people had come from Northumbria to the east a hundred or so years ago. He was aware of the strife between our two tribes in the south of the country. Mildred gave us all cups of delicious mead. We joined the others outside. Skarde was keen to be setting off for home, but Cuthbert was keen that we called in at a place called Castlerigg on our way back. It was, he said, an ancient stone circle with huge perpendicular pillars, although some had fallen. We decided to go but realized that we would not be getting back to Stedholme today. We set off through the village, attracting attention, and climbed up to the circle. It was worth the effort. The circle was the largest any of us had seen. Many stones had carvings, but we could not identify them. After looking around for half an hour, we headed back down the hill, through the town and along the lake. By 6 o'clock, we had made it down to Wigton, where we were welcome to stay.

I introduced my father to Aldheim, and they seemed to get along well. Kendra made a venison stew and vegetables, which we enjoyed. We talked a little afterwards, but we had had a long, gruelling day, and my father needed a rest. We retired to our beds when it was dark.

We were up early in the morning, washed with water from the river, and set off for Stedholme. We were home by midday, joyfully greeted by those we had left behind, particularly Megan. Nothing much had happened while we were away. A wolf had appeared on the edge of the camp, but the children had chased it away. We caught a couple of deer and a few rabbits. We had eaten some of the meat the night before. A few of the men had been out fishing and had had a good haul. Progress had been made by extending the cultivated areas, planting apple trees and an undercover of sloes and elders. The extra defence works were completed. It was all looking good.

I told Megan about the trip, meeting the Saxons at Keswick, the Roman fort and Castlerigg. She was interested in learning more about Castlerigg, but there was nothing more I could tell her. "I would like to go on one of these expeditions, but it is difficult with Dag."

"Yes, I have been feeling guilty about that," I said. "The next time you will go, and I will look after Dag."

"Maybe you could carry him in a holder on your back," she replied.

"Good idea. Next time, you might like to go to Long Meg. It is in the valley of the River Eden. You know, the one that goes through Carlisle. It is beautiful there."

"I should like that," said Megan. "Something else I should like to do is come fishing with you on the Wampool."

"Yes, we could do that," I replied.

The next few days were spent catching up on chores. Mending nets, weeding and fencing. My father was a big help, and he and Dag, my mum and Megan enjoyed each other's company a lot. We had a visit from Egil and his wife Edith and friends we had met in Holmtown. They had news from Dublin. The Celts have dominated Ireland. All the Norse men and women are now enslaved. I doubt if we would ever go back. They were also potential for invaders, so we needed to keep our defences strong.

9

C E L T I C   S I T E S

Three weeks later, we set off as a family to visit Long Meg. We could not do it in a day, so we agreed to go to Wigton first and stay with Aldheim then join the River Eden in Carlisle and then follow the Eden up to Long Meg, beyond Lazonby. We would stop off again at Wigton on the way back and show my parents Old Carlisle, which we had been impressed with. That night, we stayed with Aldheim and Kendra. We were becoming close as a family, and Dag was spoiled with the attention he got from both sets of grandparents.

We set off to Carlisle the following day. We got there at about 11 am. We went to the marketplace and the cathedral, which appeared even more impressive than before. These Christian buildings were new to my parents though they had seen similar ones in Ireland, and they found them fascinating. The cathedral priest, Patrick, told us the history of Christianity in the area. He mentioned St Bega, who had also fled from Ireland to land at the sandstone headland, now called St Bees Head. Here, she had built a cell in a grove on the seashore. Fearing attack by pirates and losing her virginity, she fled to Northumbria. A more local saint was Herbert, whose life was chronicled by Bede. Herbert was a friend of St Cuthbert, became an anchorite and lived on an island on Derwentwater. He ate the vegetables he grew and the fish from the lake. "You could visit the remains of his hermitage if you wish," said Patrick.

"These Celtic saints were considered inferior as after the Synod of Whitby, they split with the Roman Church, which had a monopoly until then. Following the Synod, the Celtic Church calculated Easter, which commemorated the crucifixion of Christ, in a different way, and the monks cut their hair differently. There was, hence, a split between the churches from then on. It sounded rather petty to me, but I was beginning to think that both the pagan and Christian religions had problems. Megan thought Herbert's life was fascinating and wanted to go to his island someday. I reluctantly agreed to take her.

After Patrick's discourse, we viewed the wooden fort and the Roman remains to the north. We then headed south along the river. It was a nice walk with sandstone cliffs and rapids. There were wooden houses with thatched roofs and well-tilled land alongside. Much of the land, though, was wooded, and we could see wolves peering out at us from within. This part of our journey took three hours until the sandstone pillars of Long Meg came into view. We were tired when we arrived, and Dags and Helga were pleased to rest and eat some cold chicken, bread and butter. We drank from the river, which was a little sandy but clean. Dag Junior went for a paddle with Megan.

After eating and resting, we wandered over to the stones, more than I had anticipated. The monument was circular, like Castlerigg. Twenty stones were upright, with many more fallen. Long Meg herself was the tallest at about eight ells tall. Marks were carved into the sandstone, which looked like cups, and we saw some rings and a spiral of circles gradually becoming smaller. Eleven stones sat in an inner circle, twelve ells in diameter, with a mound in the middle and more stones forming a grave. These were of a harder rock. Pieces of pottery and bone were lying around.

Long Meg itself was roughly square, with the four corners facing north, south, east, and west. Long Meg, it is said, lines up with the centre of the circle and the midwinter sunset. The Druids, the Celtic religious group who had built this monument, were brilliant mathematicians whose education lasted twenty years. They had built straight roads, much like the Romans did over a thousand years later, but theirs follow meridian lines all over Europe. The main meridian line through our country came from our southern coast through Cumbria via a line of hill forts through the county and up onto the west coast of Skotland.

Megan and Ingrid were fascinated by the circle of stones and would have liked to stay longer. There was a fine freshwater spring on the north side of the circle where we refilled our flasks. We then set off back down the Eden to Caer Luel. The river is navigable here, and we could have paddled down if we had had a boat. From Caer Luel, we decided to go a different way back to Stedholme. From the Market Cross, we headed past the main church and then west for a rost through a new part of town before heading northwest towards the Roman Wall, which we joined at Burgh. We then followed the wall with the estuary on one side and the marsh on the other, passing several farms until we reached a point where there was a path through the marsh, which took us on the last leg of our journey to Stedholme.

We got home around 6 pm. Agnetha prepared us our fish and broth supper. Asger called over to ask how it had gone and whether it was worth visiting. We told him it was and that we had enjoyed ourselves. Then, as we were all tired, we went to bed.

The following morning, we slept in until 9 am. Megan and I were up first. We roused the kids, got them dressed and fed them their porridge. I walked across to Asger and asked him how things had been. "We have been fine," he said. "We caught sight of Norse in the Solway, but they headed up to Caer Luel and did not come here. It does show, though, that we must keep alert and have our sentries in position day and night.

I nodded. "What would you like me to do today?"

"You can take a stint on sentry duty this morning, and in the afternoon, maybe you could teach the kids some navigation."

"Right," I said, "I will get out my sunstone and start thinking about the best way to do it." I brought out the sandstone disc and pointer and took them down to the boat by the Wampool. I relieved Aelfric, one of the guards. There was no one on the horizon, so I set up my sandstone disc and adjustable pointer, estimated the time and set a northwesterly course. Good, I still remember.

Surie, the remaining guard, and I talked while keeping watch. He was younger than me and had lost his parents and a brother in Dublin and another brother when the pirates attacked. He was understandably bitter about what had happened. "Nothing can be done about the past," I said, "It is the future that matters."

"I have met a girl from our group," Surie said. "She is very lovely, and I think we will get married."

"Excellent," I responded. "If you are sure about her, do not waste time. Get married and have children. It is the way forward."

He nodded. "That is the way I am thinking," he said.

After midday, Bjorn replaced Surie, who brought twenty children with him for their lesson. I sat them around in a circle and then called them to order. I showed them the sunstone and explained how you used the shadow to set the course and then the pointer to show the direction. I was curious to know how much they had taken in, so I called them up one at a time to demonstrate. The girls were better than the boys, which was interesting. It took about an hour, and I could see they had had enough by then. "Tomorrow, I shall take you out in the boat five at a time, and you can demonstrate what you have learned," I said. That would separate those who had been concentrating from those who have not. "See you tomorrow."

I stayed on watch until I was relieved at supper time. I returned to the langhus and had supper with Megan, Dag Junior, my parents, and Wars and Toke. We then played board games until 8 pm when we put the children to bed. Megan and I talked to my parents about their hopes for the future. We asked them to stay with us and help with the children and general life with the tribe as they had done in Dublin, which they said would be delighted to do.

The next morning, after breakfast, I walked down to the Wampool and made the boat ready for the children's navigational lesson. They arrived promptly, and I divided them into two groups of five. I gave them a brief recap on navigation before we boarded, and then I and the first group set off rowing down the river to the bay. As soon as we entered the broad expanse of water, I gave the oldest, Sten, the sandstone disc and pointer. Gertrud oversaw the tiller, and Thorwald took the main sail. We were soon sailing across the bay. I told Gertrud to steer towards the Skinburness Spit, where there had been a Roman fort. She did so competently, and we landed safely on the beach.

I had heard that the name Skinburness was haunted, but I did not believe in ghosts, so I did not mention it to the children. It had a great pebbled beach, and the kids asked if they could swim. I said they could, so they stripped off their clothes and, a little bashfully, went in to swim to shrieks from the girls as the boys splashed them. After ten minutes, they stopped for the day and returned to shore to dry themselves with grass. They dressed, and we ate our cheese and bread rolls and drank our water on the beach. We then got back on board. This time, I asked the second group to take charge. Idunn was to take the helm and Njal to steer. We headed back across the bay, passed the entrance to the Waver, and found the Wampool. We lowered the sail, and Erland and Arne rowed back to our wharf. It was 4 pm when we got back, but it had been a good day. They were a good bunch of children.

That night, after supper, we played more games, which Erik and Ingrid were getting into. Our two cats had their mad half-hour chasing each other around the langhus, which amused all the children. The cats were important members of the household. It was their job to kill mice and rats. They got on well with the puppy, Inga. The children had been to school today with Brona in charge, and she had been putting them through their paces in reading and writing. Erik found it hard, but Ingrid enjoyed it. They first learned stories about the pagan gods Odin and Freya. They were told stories about Viking heroes Erik the Red and Ragnar Lodbrok. The bible stories about Jesus Christ and the Old Testament were introduced. One or two monks and Christian preachers had taught Brona and the other teachers about the Old and New Testaments. Megan and I were happy about this. To be well-educated about these matters was important. We were different from other parents in that we thought it was just as important for Ingrid to be educated as Erik. We knew their lives would be different. Erik would be a fighting and hunting man while Ingrid would work in the home, baking, sewing, and looking after the children.

Nevertheless, we thought that both should know the basics of all skills. So, they would both be taught how to fish, how to sew, how to navigate, how to milk cows, look after horses and grow crops. Both

Megan and I had followed that rule, and it had worked for us and would work for our children.

There were going to be two more weddings in the camp. Surie was getting married to Brenda, and Skarde to Cyneburg, a girl from the Saxon tribe. Brenda and Surie will be wed in our camp and Skarde and Cyneburg in Wigton. Brenda and Surie were having a pagan wedding, while Skarde and Cyneburg would have a Christian wedding in the church in Wigton. This mix of pagan and Christian seemed to be working out alright. The weddings would be on different Saturdays; therefore, guests could go to both, and there would be two sets of celebrations. Excellent. The first Saturday would be in two weeks, and the next the following Saturday.

10

STEDHOLME DEVELOPMENTS

In the meantime, I was teaching more student sailors how to navigate and build boats. I was also with Skarde, helping him instruct in the arts of warfare—sword fighting and archery. The children were also learning how to make bows and arrows. Sword-making was a specialist skill carried out by one or two people in the tribe. A forge had to be made by the blacksmith, who in our case was Bjorn and his assistant Sten. They had built a forge in a stone building outside the langhus. It had a steel anvil, a heat shield of soapstone and a slate hearthstone. The bellows were of wood and leather, and we used charcoal as the fuel. Bjorn produced high-quality steel for our swords. Steel strands were woven to create swords that would not break in combat as many of our early swords had done. We found that mixing the bones of our ancestors with iron produced steel of a much higher quality. We did not know whether this was the actions of our ancestors giving their strength to the metal or whether something in the bone itself had this effect.

Meanwhile, Megan taught the girls cooking and sewing in the langhus kitchen. We had the benefits of their practice cooking at night for supper, which we appreciated, though occasionally we got their mishaps instead.

I went fishing most days and took Erik and one of the other boys. Occasionally, we saw other sails, but not often. One day, however, was different. Three sails appeared and headed our way. I put up full sail and headed up the Wampool estuary. Our two lookouts, Skarde and Bjorn, had already spotted the invaders and had given them the warning. Erik and I landed and headed to the village. Asger had the defences marshalled and, when we were all inside, the gates were pulled to. We positioned our bowmen on the perimeter platform, and the women put buckets of water on the fire to boil. The invaders, who numbered about sixty, walked up from the river in single file, led by a large blond bearded man with a sword and shield and bows and arrows. The children were hiding for safety in the langhus with the women. It was a terrifying situation. Their leader yelled up to Asger. "Surrender, or you are doomed."

"Never!" shouted back Asger. "We will never surrender. We know what would happen to us."

The invaders crouched low and covered their bodies with their shields. Asger waited until they got to the wall and then signalled to the women who threw the pails of boiling water on the men below. There were screams from those who had been scalded, and they retreated from our wall.

So far, so good. The attackers moved to the east side of the wall and tried again. They seemed to have worked themselves up into a frenzy, beating their chests and shrieking like men possessed. Two attempted to climb the wall again, but they had boiling water poured on them. As arrows flew from our bowmen, they retreated to regroup. It seemed they would try again, this time from the south. First, they sent a shower of arrows over the wall, but we suffered no casualties. Flaming arrows soared towards our langhus, but they missed or fell short. Their leader brandished his sword and leapt at the wall. Asger waited until he reached the top and dealt him a major blow, carving his head in two. It was over. The leader's son gathered his body and dragged him back to their boat. The rest of the men followed. We were safe, for now!

Asger gave the signal and we put down our weapons and cheered. The defeated men quarrelled with one another, scrambled into their three boats, and rowed down the river to the estuary. But we could never be confident they would not return.

Megan and I looked at each other, and we hugged the children. Asger gathered the village together, and we clapped each other on the back and vowed we would celebrate the victory that night. Avery and Thorwald replaced Skarde and Bjorn on watch at the river. The rest of us went into the langhus and lay on our beds exhausted. It had been grim, but we had got through it and triumphed, and now we would celebrate.

That night, we did have a good party. The children joined in with goat's milk, not beer. Megan and I got quite drunk, and we tumbled to bed, too inebriated to make love.

The following morning, we gave thanks to Odin and Freya, our patron, for our deliverance. Everything had worked to plan. We each had played a part, and the children had learnt valuable lessons in defending their settlement, which hopefully would serve them well in the future.

That day, we all did whatever we wanted to do. Megan, the children, and I walked out to the coast to see if we could see any porpoises and whales. We saw none but walked along the marsh back towards Skinburness and the Roman remains. I told the children Viking stories about sea monsters—the Kraken, a giant octopus, which appeared off the coast of the lands to the north, and Jormungandr, an unfathomably enormous serpent who dwells in the world sea. Then there was Huldra, a beautiful woman with long blond hair. She wore a crown of flowers, but she had the tail of a cow. She had a passion for unmarried men and would try to seduce them and take them off into the mountains. She would not let them go unless they married her. We warned Erik to be on the lookout for her. "I don't think she will fancy him," teased Ingrid. Erik blushed.

"Do not worry, Erik. I am certain some pretty girl will fancy you." Said Megan reassuringly.

When we got home, we had bread and cheese to eat and milk to drink and sat around to talk about the events of the day before. The general feeling was that things had gone well. The defences to the fort had stood up, and each of us had done the job we had trained for. The gods had looked after us.

In a few days it would be Skarde and Cyneberg and Surie and Brenda's turn to get married. Preparations were well underway. Skarde and Cyneburg were getting married in Wigton, and Surie and Brenda here in Stedholme. Megan and the other women had been helping with making the clothes. On Friday, Skarde set off for Wigton. He was looking forward to receiving his new sword. Surie was having a new sword made by Aelfric. It would be made with the ground bones of his dead father, and so it would make him brave, as his father was a great warrior, and the sword would never break.

Megan, the children, and I were going to Skarde's wedding as he was a special friend. We set off on Onsdag early in the morning. Agneta came too, as she was fond of Skarde and got on well with Cyneburg. We stayed at Aldheim's and paid a visit to St Mary's to re-familiarise ourselves with the building and the ceremony. Skarde was already there. He had come a day early to make sure he had understood the part he had to play. Ingrid and Cyneberg's younger sister Frigg were bridesmaids. It was their first time, so they were excited. Their bouquets of lilies were ready. At around 10 am, the groom and his party and Cyneberg's father and mother, Chad and Ethel, entered the church and were greeted by Aldheim. They took their seats in front of the altar. At 10.30, Skarde and Cyneburg arrived and proceeded down the aisle to the altar, followed by Ingrid and Frigg. They looked beautiful, and Megan and I were very proud of Ingrid; she looked quite the adult.

After the ceremony, the bride and groom left the church, met by a crowd of well-wishers. Skarde and Cyneberg smiled and thanked them and threw coins. Cyneberg threw her bunch of flowers, which, this time, was caught by a young Saxon girl we had not met before. That night, we all attended the celebratory dance and party—a good time had by all!

We got back to Stedholme that evening, ate supper and went to bed. We were up early the following morning to make a reasonable start. After breakfasting and dressing the children, we went to see how Surie and Brenda were getting along. Surie was so proud of his new sword, which he would present to Brenda's father, Garald, and Brenda of the dress which Agneta had made. Surie's sword was around two ells long, of sharp, tough steel, with the hilt wrapped in cow leather. The wedding was on Tysdagr, and Surie had asked Bjorn to be his best man.

Erik and Ingrid stayed at home, looked after by Agneta and my parents. We set off on Manadagr early in the morning and arrived around noon. Again, we were warmly welcomed by Aldheim, this time with Garald. Megan and I had our midday meal outside before we went into the langhus and had a nap. We were both tired and wanted to rest well before the festivities tonight. Surie and Garald exchanged swords; the one Surie received was also of excellent quality. There was then beer and French red wine to be quaffed. Megan and I got a little tipsy, but we still managed to make love when we got beneath the bearskin.

The following morning, we went down to the church. Surie received his final instruction from Aldheim, and Brenda had the final adjustments to her embroidered linen dress. Again, there was a crowd outside St Mary's. They raised a cheer when they saw the wedding party. Surie and Bjorn had taken their places at front of the church, and we took the pew behind. Brenda made her entrance and looked beautiful, escorted by her youngest sisters, Brona and Colley. Aldheim said his piece, the vows were made, and the bride was kissed, and we all retired for the wedding meal. It was a wonderful spread. Brenda's mum had done her proud. The meal was raucous, with rude speeches from the men and blushes from Brenda and her bridesmaids. The older women had seen it all before and smiled wryly. We all retired around midnight.

We said goodbye to Aldheim the next day and headed home. We were met by extremely excited villagers. Another Norse invasion had been attempted, but they had been driven off. They had sailed further back down the coast, as far as the River Waver. We resolved not to allow them to settle. Asger called a Council of War. "We need to chase them away," he said. "If they settle, they will always be close enough to launch an attack." We all agreed.

Our first action was to send two scouts to check whether the newcomers were beside the Waver. Odjer and I volunteered, though I could see that Megan was worried. We opted to wait until the following day. We had our supper of venison and retired early. Megan was warm and loving, and we hugged for a long time after making love.

11

Odjer and I set off in the morning, started up the Wampool for two rosts, and then headed west through the woods and across the marsh to where we knew the Waver lay. It was a long walk across the marsh, and it took about an hour before we reached the banks of the Waver. We descended to the stream's east bank as quietly as we could. It was not as big as the Wampool, but there were still large trout, perhaps even sea trout.

There were marshes on each side, so visibility was good, and we had to stay low. After twenty minutes, we heard a Norse voice. We flattened ourselves on the ground and crawled forward. About 50 faomrs ahead, we saw around twenty men standing in a circle around a fire. We thought it was worth risking crawling a little farther, but we were wrong. One of them turned and saw us. He gesticulated to the others. There was a yell, and they ran towards us, brandishing weapons. We scrambled up and ran back up the riverbank and into the marsh. I was just ahead of Odjer. Suddenly, there was a shout. He had tripped and fallen. Without hesitation, I turned to help him. The first of them was on us almost immediately. He did not attack but remained beside us until his compatriots caught up.

A man, who was their leader, came forward. "Who are you?" he said gruffly.

"We are Norse, like you," I replied. "We escaped from Dublin several months ago when it was captured by the Celts and sailed here."

"Where are you living now?"

I was wary of telling him exactly where we were, so I said, "Six rost in that direction." I pointed southwest.

"We met people yesterday over in that direction. Was that you?"

"No," I said, "we were over in the Saxon village of Wigton at a wedding."

"Do you find the Saxons friendly?" the man asked.

"Yes," I replied, "they are. I am aware of the problems with Alfred and our tribe in the south. But that does not concern us. Here, we intermarry; I am married to a Saxon."

The man looked thoughtful, but his men appeared restless. "Tie them up," he said, and bring them to the boat. We will decide then what to do."

Two of his men bound us. Luckily, we had no weapons with us, so we appeared peaceful. As we walked with them, joined by a rope, I tried to engage with the man who had hold of me by asking their leader's name and where they were from. But he would have none of it and pulled the noose tighter. Things were not looking good. We were quickly back beside the Waver, where they had moored their boat. They tied us separately to a tree on the bank. Those on the vessel came to look at us. Their leader arrived, discussed with his men, and then approached me.

"We have decided to spare you," he said, "providing you take us to your tribe and introduce us to your chief." This was a bit tricky, but we could buy ourselves some time. It might be possible to escape into the marsh or to learn more about them and win them over. Meanwhile, they gave us bread, and we lay down to wait until they were prepared. Eventually, they were ready to set off. Their leader, whose name I had learnt was Birger, led the way into the marsh. They had no horses or other animals, which I thought strange. Odjer and I were in the middle of the group, flanked by our captors. No escape was possible yet. The group looked from side to side, searching for other signs of life on the marsh; there was nothing but wildfowl.

We reached the Wampool and headed downstream towards Stedholme. When Birger saw the timber walls of the fortress, he recognized it immediately. "Were you trying to fool me?" he growled. "This is where we were the other day."

"I did not know. I swear," I lied.

"Huh, well, we are here now. Call your chief."

Asger had been warned of our arrival and had ensured the fortress gates were closed and the archers were ready. "Who is your chief?" he shouted.

"I am!" cried back Birger. "Open your gates, or we will kill these men." They dragged us forward and threw us onto the ground.

"And if we open the gates, we will all be killed, every man, woman and child," responded Asger.

"I promise that will not be the case," replied Aelbric. It seemed like a stalemate.

"I cannot risk it," said Asger.

"Then they will die in front of their wives and children," shouted Birger, taking out his knife and putting it to Odjer's throat.

"Wait." retorted Asger. "Can we reach some agreement? What is it that you really want from all of this? You could end up losing your prisoners and not gaining any conquest. Surely, we can work something out from which we can both learn. There is room for all of us in this country. You are camped near the Waver, like us near the Wampool. There is very little settlement in that area."

Birger was thoughtful. "Let us talk more," he said. "Perhaps one of my men and I could come into your fortress to talk with you."

"Brun, whom you hold a prisoner, is my top adviser," said Asger. "Release him if you want to talk."

"If I do, then you must give me someone in exchange," responded Aelbric.

"I shall give some thought to that," replied Asger, and he stepped away from the gates to consult with the men behind him. Meanwhile, Odjer and I waited nervously. We both had families who depended on us.

Shortly, Asger reappeared. "This man, Bjorn, will take Brun's place," he shouted. "But woe betide that any harm should befall him."

"You have my word," shouted back Birger.

And so, I was released and walked to the fort gates, and Bjorn, looking apprehensive, came towards me. I embraced him, and he smiled grimly and walked down to the tree where I had been to have his hands tied behind his back. Meanwhile, Birger had asked his key adviser, Arthur, to join him and walk to the gates. They opened, and Birger and Arthur walked in. Asgar and I met them and led the way to the fireplace, where we sat down. Megan brought us beer to drink, and I introduced her to Birger and Arthur, who were very courteous to her. She then retired, and Asgar opened the conversation with an account of how we had arrived at Stedholme. Birger then explained how they had lived in Norway and set sail via Dublin to come to Britain's west coast, partly for adventure and partly for a new life and a new place to live. They were not welcome in Dublin, so they travelled here.

We talked for a while, and there were no significant elements of disagreement. Birger would settle with his tribe in the Waver basin, two rosts west of Wigton. They would use the Waver for navigation and build a langhus and a fort, or at least a defensive wall. We would introduce them to the Saxons we knew. We could also supply them with young cattle, sheep, and poultry. All four of us shook hands. It was a successful meeting. Birger and Arthur left by the front gate, smiling. They returned to their tribe, and after a brief discussion, Bjorn was released. Birger's tribe left to head back to the Waver and start building the langhus. Bjorn joined us in the fort and related his experience. They had treated him firmly but fairly. That was fine.

Megan, Erik, Ingrid, and I settled back down to our routine. Up around 8.30, breakfast at 9, and then, for Erik and Astrid, it was the runic alphabet or whatever academic studies Agneta had planned. In the afternoon, practical skills were taught, sewing and weaving for the girls and fishing and sailing for the boys. There was also hunting, and blacksmithing with Alfric and Sten and whatever other practical skills Agneta felt we needed to learn—time passed quickly.

We kept in touch with Birger, Arthur, and their tribe, and they also met up with the Saxons from Wigton. We had a strong community group on the Solway plain, which would not easily fall apart and could overcome any future invasions. However, I guess that the previous tribes of Celts, and indeed the Romans, had also felt the same way. In fact, what had happened to the Celts? The nearest Celtic fort had been on Carrock Fell, on the northern fringe of the Lake District. It was in ruins now but must have once been very impressive, as had the Celts themselves. They, and particularly the Druids, had been awe-inspiring with their stone circles, oppidums and twenty years of education. I thought it would be a good idea to visit Carrock Fell with our tribe one day. I would talk about it to Asger.

12

I talked to Asger about Carrock Fell the next day. He was all for it and said he would like to come himself. I thought it would be nice to invite Dag and Helga, Asger and his wife Brenda and Skarge and Cyneberg. We set off on Frjadagr, the men leading the way up the Wampool to Wigton, Brocklebank, through the Saxon village of Caldbeck and then through Hesket New Market. We followed directions from Aldheim and took Carrock Beck through a wooded valley onto Carrock Fell. Aldheim told me that the Fell had been mined for minerals. The Romans had opened the first mines, and the Saxons took over when the Romans left. They had all mined the mountain for copper and lead. The locals had made jewellery from copper and gold found there. There would likely be some locals up there today.

Sure enough, we came across a mine worked by Celtic locals. They had a different attitude to those in Dublin and were friendly. Three families were there, and they had mined this shaft since Roman times and made jewellery on-site. Megan was intrigued, and even Astrid showed interest.

"I would like a ring. Can we afford it?" asked Megan. I looked in my purse. I had a few penningars.

"How much are the rings?" I asked the man who was selling the jewellery.

"They are one hundred penningars each," he said. "I can do you a deal if you would like one for your daughter.

Astrid seemed keen, so I said, "I will give you one hundred and fifty for two rings."

"One hundred and seventy-five," he countered.

"Done." I agreed.

"Give me a couple of hours, and I will have them made to fit," he promised. "Would you like one?" he queried.

"No thanks," I retorted. "You have bankrupted!"

I asked if we could go down the shaft. Megan, Embla and Cyneberg were not interested, but Skarde, Dag Senior and the children were. We borrowed a tallow lamp from Aidan, one of the miners. I crouched down low and led the way through the shaft entrance and down the passage which was about three ells high. The floor was uneven, and there were pools of water and clouds of dust. The roof had pine posts supporting it and pine planks across. I was glad to see that the wood was stout and sound. We got to the working face about twenty faomrs in. I could see copper and another mineral alongside it, which Aidan told me was tungsten. I picked up a piece of rock with both minerals as a keepsake, and Erik and Ingrid did the same. Soon, we turned around and set off back to the way we had come. We emerged into bright daylight and met our group. The children showed their mineral keepsakes to Megan, who was impressed that they had managed to do it. They were growing up.

We carried on further up the Fell. It was one of those climbs where you were always going over a rise and thinking you were getting to the top, but you were not; there was another horizon. We stopped occasionally to rest and look back and enjoy the view north and west over towards Wigton and the Sulwath plain to Stedholme. You could almost imagine you could see the people there, but you could not. You could see wisps of smoke spiralling out of the trees and the church towers of St Mary's. The Rivers Waver and Wampool were visible, and the Ehen further west. The smoke of Carlisle was also visible, and further north, the bluish mountain of Criffel. It was magnificent.

"Not bad," I said to Asgar,

"No, it is spectacular. It was a lucky choice we made coming here."

Our group continued to Wigton, and we had a brief meeting with Aldheim. We then moved on towards Stedholme. There, we were greeted by the rest of the tribe. Life had carried on as normal. Agneta and Brona had continued educating the children; Erik and Ingrid would have some catching up to do I should talk to Brona and find out what they missed and if they could get some extra help.

Tilling of the land, fishing and hunting had continued. It was now late Heyannir and time to harvest the oats we had sowed in spring. We had planted about an arkriengd of land and sowed the seed by hand. We were going to plant our wheat in mid-, so we began to prepare another arkriengd of land. We chose the most fertile, deepest soil we could find. Our blacksmith, Bjorn, had made an ard for us like we had in Dublin, and we ploughed the land. We then raked it with tools made by Aelfric, ready to scatter the wheat seed in September.

13

W O L V E S !

Megan and I had noticed wolves on the outskirts of our camp early in the mornings. Wolves had a special place in Norse society. They were the subject of stories, especially around the campfire during late winter nights. We had over fifty sea wolf stories. Sea wolves, or werewolves, are divided into ranks in order of strength and fierceness. There are five ranks, with Alpha being the top and Gamma the lowest. One of the most famous tales is of Sigmund and Sinfjotli. Wolves stalk the edges of our territory. They are destroyers and are at their strongest when we are at our weakest. Wolves are the enemy of man. They are exiled from our world, and whereas we consider family and social ties to be particularly important, being isolated from the tribe was almost a sentence of death.

When someone in Viking society had killed a member of the tribe, they would be strung up by the heels alongside a live wolf because they had acted as a wolf by killing one of its members. Even so, Viking society worked like a wolf society where powerful alpha males sometimes work together. The stories that we told were steeped in blood feuds and disputes between Viking chieftains. One wolf god was Fenrir, the son of Loki, the trickster god, and the giantess Angrboda. At Ragnarok, the end of time, it was said that the chains will be burst, and the wolf would run free. At Ragnarok, Fenrir will consume the sun and kill Odin, the king of the gods. Wolves, though, as well as ravens, are dedicated to Odin. Viking sagas tell of Odin worshipping warrior bands known as "ulfeonar", biting their shields and howling savagely and fighting with their fingernails. They felt no pain in battle. They wore wolfskins as protection instead of armour and built themselves up into a frenzy before battle until they believed they were invincible.

The warriors became so excited by the love of fighting that they began attacking their own men. A famous poem describes the situation as follows:

> *Wolf-coats they call them that in battle*
> *Bellow into bloody shields*
> *They wear wolves' hides when they come into the fight*
> *And clash their weapons together*

Megan and I knew the poem from way back but had not found it very appealing. But the whole wolf element, the stories and garb, created a frightening image of us as terrifying, almost feral, warriors. Megan and I did not see ourselves as being like that at all, nor had we taught our children this type of culture. I am sure we would not have been able to develop the friendships we had with our Saxon friends, and more recently Celtic, if that had been the case. We had many carvings of wolf heads on our weapons and staves. However, the image we had and still have of the Viking colonists ravaging other civilisations is gradually changing, and we are becoming a much more civilized, peace-loving race. We shall see! In the meantime, the wolves had disappeared from view, deterred by our barking dogs.

14

E R I K   A N D   I N G R I D

Our two children continued to grow and learn. Erik had taken an interest in horses and was learning to look after the horse we had brought from Dublin. He had had lessons from Arne and could trot, canter and gallop, which was surprisingly good as he was only six. He liked to go with his friend Thorwau, Bjorn's son and a couple of years older. They liked to take the horse down to the marsh and exercise it there, where it was flat and free from obstacles. They had to be careful not to fall into crevices and of the tides that came in very quickly there. The boys would gather mushrooms at the marsh, which pleased Megan and Bjorn's wife, Liv, as they made a welcome addition to our diet. They also picked brambles and sloes, which we ate after the main course and added interest to our meals.

Ingrid had developed her musical talent from what her mother had taught her in Dublin. She had a fine voice and was learning to play the flute. We had no time to bring anything like that when we fled, but we had made them from walnut wood we found in the nearby forest. Aslos was exceptionally talented at making musical instruments, and he had been making flutes of various kinds, a lyre, a talharpa with strings of horsehair, and more recently, drums with the beating surface of pig hide.

Ingrid was diligent and was practising currently. I went to hear her in the corner of the langhus with her teacher, Freya. The music they were playing was a folk song about a beautiful milkmaid who falls in love with a warrior lost in battle. However, she bears his son, who eventually avenges his father. Most of our songs are dark and violent, but this one was more subtle.

Ingrid was concentrating hard, and we sat down quietly in the corner. The flute sound was incredibly beautiful, and Ingrid played it intently. Freya was nodding appreciatively and smiled at us when we sat down. They were coming to the end of the lesson. Freya signalled that there was just one more tune. It was a folk song we had not heard before called "The Rose Garden", which, as you can imagine, is about roses in a garden. The gardener plants lilies, and there is a battle between the two flowers about who can attract the most bees and, hence, make the most mead. It was a pretty song, and we really enjoyed it. "Where does it come from?" I asked Freya.

"From France," she said. "Where else? They always have the most interesting and tuneful songs."

We nodded our appreciation of it. It ended after a few minutes, and we went over to Ingrid. She smiled and said, "Thank you for coming to hear me. I really enjoyed the session."

Freya said, "She is progressing very well, and I am considering introducing her to more difficult music." She continued, "We are having a concert later in the year, and I think she is good enough to play a part."

"That is wonderful," Megan said. "We shall certainly come along."

All three of us strolled back to our section of the langhus where Agnetha was taking care of Dag. He was ready for a feed, so Megan lowered her dress and gave him one of her nipples.

After Dag's feed, Ingrid played with him. He loved that, especially when he was tickled. Megan smiled and said, "Let us have supper. I have stew and bread left over."

"That will be fine," I said, fetching the cutlery for the meal and placing it on the table. "Shall we see if my parents would like to join us?" I asked.

"Why not," replied Megan. So, I went to find them. My father was outside watching Aelfric beating out a sword. It was for another wedding: one of our boys to a Saxon girl.

"Time for supper, Dad," I said. "Where is mum?"

"She has gone for a walk by the river," he said. "I will fetch her."

I returned to the langhus and informed Megan what was happening. "I am pleased," she said. "I want us all to stay close." Dag and Helga arrived a few minutes later and sat down to their stew. We had apple and pastry pie for our pudding. I looked around; we were one happy family.

The following day, we thought we would all go for a walk together, so we decided to visit our Norse brothers on the Waver to see how they were getting on. We arrived around midday, and they were pleased to see us. They had been busy learning to fish the Waver and had sailed down the river and across to Scoti. They had sailed up the River Annan to where my parents had come from. They had also made friends with our Saxons, including Aldheim in Wigton, and had been introduced to their Christian ways.

The Celts worshipped many gods, particularly, Mercury, who they regarded as inventor of the arts and the god of commerce, especially travellers and merchants. After Mercury, the Gauls, or Celts, honoured Apollo, who drove away diseases; Mars, who controlled war; Jupiter, who ruled the heavens; and Minerva who was into handicrafts. When the Romans conquered the Celts, they adopted their gods. Aldheim's Christianity fascinated them, as it differed from the old gods. Jesus, especially, gave them food for thought as a god who had come to earth had been crucified and intended to come again. The miracles were also fascinating, and his moral code of being helpful to one's neighbour was appealing. The Celts had settled in well. I am sure that will eventually mean more intermarriage, which can only be for the good. We chatted more about Alfred, but they had heard no more than we had. None of them wanted to get involved as there was enough to do to bring up our families and develop our land and buildings here. We talked about our visit to Carrock Fell and the mine, and they thought they would go too.

We had a light meal of fruit and nuts with them before returning to Stedholme. Megan soon had a meal ready, and we sat down to enjoy it. For a change, we had herring, sauce and carrots. For dessert, we had apples, raspberries and bilberries, and afterwards, a few walnuts. I sometimes wondered what had happened to the three slaves we had had in Dublin, Idunn, in particular, but also Calder and Aslos. There was nothing we could do now, but maybe something might occur in the future. There was talk amongst the Norse warriors about retaking Dublin. As it was, we had no slaves with us now, and we were restricted in our ambitions as a result. I decided I would chat with Asger about the possibility of us acquiring slaves tomorrow.

15

SLAVES AND CAMP LIFE

The following day, I found Asger outside, near Aelfric, the toolmaker's building. I waited until they finished talking and then opened the conversation with Asger. He listened, I thought, sympathetically. Aelfric was also listening.

"Yes," said Asger, "I had slaves in Dublin for the same purpose as you. Life over here is different somehow. We should continue to talk about it with the others and have a Thing meeting when it could be decided upon."

"It would help me," chipped in Aelfric. "I could certainly do with extra hands. It is a lot of work for me when I am on my own. A female companion would be an asset too." He grinned as he said this.

"I doubt she would be making rakes much," I said.

"Happy?" said Asger as we walked away.

"Yes," I replied. "We will see how it goes."

I went back to Megan and told her what we had been discussing. "We have slaves in Wigton," she said. "They fulfill the same role as your slaves did in Dublin, but I don't want another Idunn here!" I nodded.

"No chance of that, Megan," I said quickly. I would mention it, though, to Dag and Helga and hear what their experience in Dublin was like. Maybe it was time we started thinking about more children!

I took Erik out in our skiff down the river and up the estuary a little way. He enjoyed our time alone together. "Have you and Thorwau had the horse down to the marsh recently?" I asked.

"Yes, we had a gallop yesterday," he retorted.

"How is it going?" I asked.

"I am enjoying it, and so is Thorwau. He is a better rider than I am."

"We are all good at something," I replied. "No one is good at everything."

That night, I asked Megan whether she would like another child. "Yes," she said. "It is in the lap of the gods how many children we have. Some have none, and others have so many they cannot look after them all. We should go for two or three, so I think we should start after my next period."

"Fine," I replied. I smiled and hugged her.

I took Ingrid and Erik out in the longboat the next day. The weather was fine, and the wind was from the Southwest. We decided we would sail up the Eden to the old Roman port of Luguvallio. It was quite a trip down the Wampool out into Moricambe Bay and then the Solway, past the Sulwath ford and the haaf net fishermen and into the River Eden. We continued upstream for three sjomils, past St Ann's Well and ancient earthworks to the centre of Luguvallio.

We moored at the town dock. I took Ingrid and Erik up to the centre of town to the Market Cross. They pottered around the stalls. I gave them a few penningars and told them to spend it wisely, but I was not sure they would listen. Ingrid bought a pendant with a garnet, while Erik bought a wool sweater for the winter. We wandered up to the wooden church, a half rost from the marketplace. It was quite interesting but not very gripping for the children, so we came away and cut through the market and back to the skiff.

There were a few boats in the port, some from across the Solway and others from ports along the Solway coast. Two were selling fish and were doing a good trade. It was 4 pm by then and time to go. We jumped in, I untied the skiff, and we pushed off under the bridge and into the main stream. The current was with us, and we sped along. I pointed out where the River Caldew, which we had last encountered on Carrock Fell, joined the Eden. It was cleaner than the sandier main river. After four or five sjomils, we were out into the Solway estuary, passing the small Saxon villages along the coast. The wind was against us, as was usual in this area, and we decided to row the skiff. It took us two more hours to enter the Wampool and then berth. All three of us had enjoyed the day, and Ingrid and Erik enjoyed showing their purchases to Megan, who was suitably impressed. We had skause, or stew, for supper, which included venison and boiled and mashed carrots, cabbage and peas. For afters, we had apple and cherry pie with cream. It was delicious and well received as we had had little to eat all day. The children told their mum all about Luguvallio and the people they had met. At 8 pm, they headed to bed, as did Megan, and I followed a couple of hours later.

In the morning, after breakfast, I chatted to Asgar about our trip. He was always keen to hear about other communities, especially the non-Viking ones so that he would hear if there was any sign of discontent, which could mean trouble for us. There had been one or two longboat sails out in the Solway, which we had seen when we had walked down to the coast, but none had come up the estuary. Hopefully, word had spread that we were not to be meddled with.

We were running short of meat, so I decided to kill two birds with one stone: teach Erik hunting skills and restock the larder. I asked Skarde if he would like to come, and he said he would. We equipped ourselves with bows, arrows and spears and headed upriver for four rosts and then west out towards a large marsh called Wedholme Flow, where, it was rumoured, there were lots of deer and wild boar. We went down to the Wampool, crossed it, and headed into the marsh. We had dug peat for our fires here before. We leave the turves to dry and then collect them when they are dry and lighter. They make a decent fire, if a little smoky. We could see there were some turves left, and if we had enough manpower, we would pick them up on the way back. We followed a path that led past where we had dug the turves towards the centre of the marsh. Skarde stopped suddenly and pointed to the right. A young female deer was grazing around one hundred faomrs away. It raised its head, saw us, but did not move. We decided that Skarde would circulate to the left, get behind it and try to drive it towards us. The children and I would keep our heads down until it was close, and then I would try to shoot it with one of my arrows. Skarde bent low, scurried off and disappeared. He reappeared later, twenty faomrs behind the deer, which was still grazing. He stood up and waved, and the deer, seeing him, walked towards where we were hidden. Erik was getting excited. I got out my arrows and fitted one to my bow, still out of sight. The deer was now some fifty faomrs away and still well out of range. I was not a bad shot, but I would not hit it from where I was. We kept down and quiet. After a little more time, she was twenty faomrs away. We could see Skarde walking slowly behind her. When she was ten faomrs from me, I rose, raised my bow, and shot. I missed by a few ells. She saw me, heard the arrow whistle past and shot off to her right. Damn, I said that was not good. Skarde approached, and I sighed ruefully. "Hard luck," he said. "Let's continue further along the path and see what else we can see."

"Shame, Dad," said Erik, "better luck next time."

We vigilantly headed down the path. Suddenly, there was a grunting noise, and out of the brush charged a wild boar. It ran straight for Erik, caught him in the stomach and threw him to the ground. I drew my sword and leapt forward with a roar. I stabbed at the boar and caught him in the chest just behind his right leg. He squealed in pain and tried to rise but fell again. I pulled out my sword and caught him again, this time in the stomach. This was the final blow; he quivered and died. I turned to Erik, who was shocked but otherwise unharmed.

"Are you alright?" I asked.

"Yes, I am," he responded.

We were lucky. It was a close thing, and the outcome could have been much worse. I gave him a hug. Skarde was also shocked; it had taken him by surprise as well. At least we had got a few meals out of it. I cut a long stout pole from a hazel bush and trussed up the boar with rope. After a brief rest and a drink of water, we set off back to Stedholme. We got back around 5 pm. Erik told his story to Ingrid and Megan. Ingrid was impressed, but Megan expressed her concern. "He could have been killed," she said to me. "You need to be more careful. He is just a young boy." I said nothing. She was right. Dag and Helga also expressed their concern. I could see I was going to be the family's bad apple for a while.

The boar's head was cut off and hung on the wall of the langhus, the body skinned and cut in half. It was then put on the spit over the fire. It took an hour to cook, too late for supper, but we would look forward to enjoying it tomorrow. There was no lovemaking that night!

The following day, Megan and Ingrid went with Dag and Helga to Wigton to see her family. Skarde and I recounted yesterday's story to Asgar and the rest. At least we knew the stories of Wedholme Flow being a rich source of game were true. I weeded the garden and repaired the fencing, which took most of the day. Erik gave me a hand. As Megan and Ingrid were in Wigton, Erik and I cooked our own meals, eating more of the boar in the evening. It was tender and juicy, and I added apple sauce and cooked carrots and peas to go with it. I have to say, it was delicious.

Megan, Ingrid, and my parents were staying another night in Wigton, so I took Erik fishing on the Solway the following day. We caught several herring and some prawns, which we had for supper, and they were delicious. Erik and I had a good relationship. We were interested in and good at the same things. Like father, like son.

Megan, Ingrid, Dag and Helga arrived back from Wigton. They had been made very welcome by Aldheim and Megan's family and friends. Further relationships had developed between Saxon and Viking young men and women, and more weddings were planned. The different religions did not seem to be a problem.

Megan took me to one side after we had eaten at midday. "Can we have a talk?" she said.

"Of course," I responded. I took her arm, and we wandered down along the path to the river.

"Your father is getting a bit absent-minded, Brun. Your mother has noticed it too. Perhaps you could keep an eye on him. I know, at his age, many men and some women become like this—forget things, lose things, like he left his sandals in the house where we lodged in Wigton, and he could not remember Aldheim's name."

I scratched my head and thought hard. Now that she mentioned it, there had been a few incidents like that. He was forgetting the names of people and places, and I would notice him stumble once or twice. I said I would keep an eye on him. Megan smiled sympathetically. Her parents were a bit younger, but we knew it eventually came to every family. I would ask my mother what she thought at the right moment.

I was crossing the square outside the langhus when Asger called me over. "Good morning, Brun. I wanted to have a word with you about the discussion we had about slaves. They were very helpful in Dublin, and I have been given some thought to having six or so here. I noticed that there was a small slave market in Carlisle, and we could have a look around there for a start."

I nodded. "I have no objection myself, although it would make us a different kind of tribe," I said. "I think it would be useful if you raised it at the next Thing just to test the water."

He nodded in agreement. "I will," he said. Things were held once a week, and all the adults were invited. The next Thing was to be tomorrow night, so Asger said he would raise the subject then. I mentioned this to Megan and my father and mother. Megan was supportive, though thoughtful, but my parents were less so. They said they would attend, so it would be interesting to hear what they had to say. A vote would be taken, and a simple majority would decide the matter.

Rules would need to be drawn up: What about sexual relationships and children? How would they be owned? Where would they sleep? These thoughts filled my head that day, while I worked in the fields, weeding the peas and carrots. I could understand Megan reservations, bearing in mind my relationship with Idunn.

I took carrots and peas back to the langhus, where Megan and Helga were beginning to prepare supper. They were pleased with the carrots and peas. They washed them, cut them up and threw them in the pot. I sat down to talk to Erik and Ingrid about their day. Ingrid and her friends had been learning to sew with Agnetha, while Erik had been fishing with Thorwau and other boys down at the river. They had caught a few herring. I made a note to take him out with a haaf net later in the year when the salmon were running.

That night, Megan let me know it was a good time to try for another child. We were both still passionate, and we both climaxed. I hope we are successful. We shall be trying each night until her time is over. We slept well right through the night.

The following day, I talked through the issues around the slavery question with other members of our tribe, both male and female. There was a general feeling that it was a promising idea, but there needed to be rules. On the question of ownership, it would be the man in the household who would be the owner. Initially, they would have their own quarters within the langhus. It was accepted that some of the women slaves would be having sexual relationships with the men. If there were children, and that was inevitable, they would become part of the Norse family, and they would eat together. Eventually, some of the slaves and their children would earn their freedom.

That night after our meal, we all gathered in the langhus to try to come to a decision. Asger called us together. There were about forty of us. Asger reminded us of the situation in Dublin and pointed out that adding slaves to our tribe would make us more powerful, enable us to cultivate more land, grow more crops and catch more fish. He said that we would buy them in Carlisle, where he had seen slaves being sold the last time we had paid a visit. When he enquired, he was informed that most of the slaves came from Eastern Europe, though a few came from Egypt and were brown-skinned and others from North Africa were black.

Skarde asked, "Where would they sleep?"

"We would need to build another langhus or a few smaller houses," responded Asger.

Megan asked about the slave women taken on as prostitutes. "I think that is something that each man and his wife will need to work out for themselves," said Asger. Most people nodded at that.

"Will they eventually be entitled to their freedom?" asked Stone.

"That, again, would depend on each owner," replied Asger.

After the questions ended, Asger said, "I think we can move to a vote now. Would those in favour put up their hands?" Asger had asked me to do the counting. I counted twenty-eight hands in favour, including mine and Megan's. "Those against?" asked Asger. Ten hands went up. "Any abstentions?" Asger queried. Two raised their hands. "Then it is carried," said Asger. "Now, how many should we purchase? I suggest four men and two women." No one disagreed. "Brun and I will go up to Carlisle on the next Market Day," Asger said. "All agreed?" All hands went up. We then dispersed to our quarters.

The next Carlisle Market Day was Porsdagr, and Asger, Megan and I set off early. We went by horseback and followed the same route as we had done previously on foot. We got to Carlisle at ten and made our way up to the Market Square, fed our horses and tied them to posts near the Market Cross. The slaves were corralled into a fenced area, and there was a big crowd looking them over. There were both men and women and with one or two exceptions, all were white. There would be around fifty altogether.

One or two of the women were crying, and one had a young girl with her, presumably her daughter. We squeezed through the crowd to get to the fence and looked at the first group of men. There was one guy who was very tall and well-built. He had a dark complexion, more Iberian than Middle Eastern. He had scars on his face and shoulders. Asger looked at me, and I shook my head. There were men around the outside of the fence who were selling the slaves. We moved along the fencing and came to a group of three men and two women, one of whom had a child with her. We stopped and asked the man in charge where they were from.

"They are all from Iberia," he said. "I bought them at a port on our south coast, and they have been here at my home for two days. I am pleased with them, although the women and child are exhausted from the walking."

"What language do they speak?" I asked.

"They speak Castellano," he replied, "and a smattering of Saxon that they have picked up from me." We were familiar with Saxon but had no Castellano. So, we would have to make do and learn each other's languages as we went along.

I thought that this group were promising and said that to Asger. Asger nodded. "I agree," he said. We approached the man in charge. "We like the group of five and the girl," Asger said.

"Right," replied the owner. "You can see that they are clean and healthy. I am asking for sixty ounces of silver. The woman is a skilled cook, and the men know about fishing and hunting."

"I suggest fifty would be a fair price," responded Asger.

"I will settle for fifty-five," replied the man.

"Alright, I agree," said Asger, and they shook on the deal with their right hands. The man opened the gate in the fence, and the slaves filed out with the girl clinging to her mother, obviously nervous. Megan immediately went to the girl and her mother and embraced them. They were both dark-haired with brown skin. They smiled faintly at Megan.

"What language do you speak?" said Megan in Norse. They shook their heads. Megan tried again in Saxon, and again, there was no response. Megan then greeted them in Celtic, and there were smiles.

"Yes, I speak Celtic," the woman said. "We all do, including my daughter."

"That is a relief," replied Megan.

"My name is Beatris, and my daughter is Grana."

"I have never heard the name Grana before," said my wife,

"It is unusual," said Beatris, "but it has been in the family a long time."

I could see that Megan and Beatris would get along well, and Grana was like her mother, so that would be fine. The other woman introduced herself as Madelena, Beatris's younger sister. That was fortunate too. The three men introduced themselves as Junez, Geronimo and Ferrando. All three seemed pleasant. Junez was Beatris and Madelena's brother, so we had four slaves who were related. I thought that could be good or bad, but we would see.

We put their belongings, rugs, spare clothes, food and drink on the pack horse and set off for Wigton. I chatted to the men along the way. My knowledge of Celtic was limited, but I learned that pirates had captured them in Iberia and brought up through France to the coast where they were sold to their previous owners, who put them on a wooden sailboat and took them to the south coast of Angleland. They were marched on foot to Carlisle. It had been a hard journey, particularly for the children, but they had survived and were hoping that the next stage of their life would be happier and easier. When the slaves arrived at Stedholme, there was great excitement on both sides. Ingrid and Erik were particularly excited to meet Grana. Ingrid gave her a big hug, and Erik smiled at her shyly. She was quite pretty.

16

A NEW PHASE

Megan took Beatris, Madelena and Grana into the langhus and showed them where to wash. She had partitioned off a section of the new part of the langhus with rope and skins. She had also given them four bear-skins for bedding and told them to join us for food when they were ready. She showed them where to do their lavatory functions, a small, covered building outside. I took the men into another section of the new langhus and did the same thing.

They were pleased with the arrangements. I went back and shared this with Megan. "I think we made a good choice," she said. I went over to talk to Asger.

"I assume you would like Megan to take ownership of Beatris and Grana," I said. I can take ownership of Junez as he is Beatris's brother. What about the others?"

"Well, I thought I would take ownership of Geronimo and Skarde of Ferrando."

"Sounds good to me," I retorted. "I thought I would get Junez to help with the agricultural and fruit work. I will take him fishing as well."

"That's settled, then," said Asger. "May Odin be with us."

I told Megan what I had discussed with Asger and explained to the men what was happening. I took Ferrando to Skarde, who said he would get him to help with fishing and agriculture work, like me with Junez. Asger was already talking to Geronimo, so that was all sorted. Megan got Beatris to help with preparing the meals. Beatris had been an accomplished harpist. The instrument had been brought to Iberia by Egyptians. "She must have come from an important family. I shall have to ask her," said Megan. "We do not have a harp, but if she could describe one and how it was made, I am sure Aelfric could make one. Then Ingrid or Erik or the other children might like to learn it."

We had our first meal together that night. We ate outside on benches and chairs around a single table as it was fine. We had pork and vegetables and an excellent apple dessert. We had just enough plates and cutlery. We told Junez and Beatris about our own history from Dublin, about Helga's murder and my parents Dag and Helga escaping to Annan and their journey here.

Junez told us about being captured by pirates who had come up the River Tagus and raided their village. They had defended themselves, and many were killed. Junez, Beatris, Grana and the other men were captured, taken onboard a ship and transported to Exeter Quayside. From there, it had been a long, hard walk up to Carlisle with little to eat. From the look on her face, Megan was horrified by their story, and I could see she would be determined to ensure that our new friends— for that is how we saw them—would be well treated by us.

After our apple dessert, we all went for a walk down to the river, chatted with Chad and Edgar, who were on watch and then went on to Moricambe Bay. It was all new to Junez, Beatris and Grana, and they were quite taken with it. We ambled back and went to bed. A new chapter had begun for Stedholme.

www.ingramcontent.com/pod-product-compliance
Lightning Source LLC
Chambersburg PA
CBHW040837010826
48978CB00012BB/786